The Rise and Fall of Third Leg

Also by Jon Longhi:

Bricks and Anchors

Zucchini & other stories

The Rise and Fall of Third Leg

Stories by

Jon Longhi

keep the Faith in Port land

MANIC D PRESS
SAN FRANCISCO

for Jen

manic d press
box 410804
san francisco, ca 94141 usa

ISBN 0-916397-27-0

cover drawing: r. crumb
cover color: bob armstrong

The Rise and Fall of Third Leg

Sometimes when you're driving late at night you get so tired that the white lines look like fortunes from a fortune cookie and you're tempted to pull over and read them.

old Car

My old car started out proud and new with a polish you could actually see yourself in. It was a tank of a stationwagon handed down to me from my parents when I graduated college. But I drove it to death in midnight trips to the beach and joy rides through Philadelphia. Spun it around in a blizzard on I-95 and a Toyota truck caved in one side but it still drove. Occasionally the battery would sputter out for no reason and leave me stranded with some girl miles from anywhere in the middle of nowhere. The radio broke, the paint chipped off, you could hardly determine the original color anymore, much less the reflection of your face. The shocks were so bad that passengers bounced around like rock candy furious to get out of its box. In the fall, on its last legs, the heater broke and the rear windshield got stuck in the open position. One of the last rides was to a junkyard to help Phillip throw away his ratty furniture. You couldn't tell the difference between my car and the piles of wrecks. Looking at it rusting in that graveyard I was reminded of the year before when the brakes had gone out at a crowded intersection and I had to maneuver maniacally through a tangle of shrieking horns. But it had driven me to see The Residents and Sonic Youth. It was the ultimate pimpmobile for party trips to concerts. Back beneath the rear windshield made a perfect bed for me and a lover, and after sex we would stare up at the stars like fish in a tank.

By winter the old car refused to move. The ignition only generated a phlegmy gurgle. Slowly it sunk into the mud and rusted to pieces. When the snows fell it became a larval white cube with the gaping maw of the open rear windshield sucking in flakes; inside the seats were reupholstered in frost, the only sign of life being that, for some reason, the heat light still glowed. The thaw arrived in spring as the tires fell off and the frame filled with rainwater. The water was a foot deep in the trunk and mosquito larva and tiny fishes swam between the seats. At night you could hear frogs croaking beneath the dashboard. Flowers and ivy grew from the upholstery as butterflies spread their wings on the steering wheel. It looked like a terrarium by the time I pushed it out on the street. The police towed it to its final fate. At night I sometimes dream of my old car, reduced to orange lava in the hell of a junkyard's furnace, crushed to a nameless block of steel, reduced to its cubic essence. Or perhaps it is lying in one piece on some anonymous stack, its headlights yearning for tears, the broken windshield begging for a return of the still pond and tiny creatures which had swum its back seats.

The Invisible Baby

The bum level was getting real high at the corner of Haight and Ashbury, especially since it was Christmas and freezing cold. That night I was out putting up protest flyers against the Persian Gulf war and there was an especially odd bum on the corner. He looked like a '60s burnout who'd done way too much heroin in the '70s: tall, bearded, unbathed. You could tell he'd been on the streets for weeks, because besides the fatigue of the weather and exposure he wore an outfit of hand-me-downs that had to have been stolen from the dumpsters of local clothing stores. The uniform of the homeless. He was pushing a baby carriage with no baby in it. Instead the seat was filled with a gaudy psychedelic collection of junk one can only find leftover at Haight-Ashbury yard sales on a Sunday afternoon. Glow-in-the-dark telephones, voodoo dolls, mandalas, old hippie artwork, and a dildo shaped like Gumby. The bum had a set of battery-powered Christmas tree lights draped over his shoulders.

And he pushed his baby carriage down the street going, "Spare any change for the invisible baby tonight? Can you spare a quarter for the invisible baby?"

Sometimes a passerby would look down at the seat and say, "No, sorry, not tonight," as if there was really something there. But for the most part everyone walking past on the sidewalk just ignored him completely, turning their eyes away and walking on by as if he didn't even exist.

What he should have been saying was, "Spare any change for the invisible man?"

Lousy Neighbors

When we lived in the Haight there were these guys in the apartment above us who dove headfirst into the whole modern primitives thing. They had multiple body piercings, who knows what was under their clothes, and their faces alone had dozens of orifices where none should have been. When you talked to them it was really hard to keep eye contact because you'd always keep focusing in on that big dangly piece of jewelry hanging from their eyebrows or nose.

After awhile we began referring to our neighbors as the Tackle Box Faces. We made jokes about how it would take them forever to get through airport security. Even after they had filled up a bowl with earrings the little metal detector wand would keep going crazy squealing as the security guard passed it over their crotches.

The Tackle Box Faces were loud motherfuckers who played out of tune punk rock versions of the Spiderman theme song on stereos where the volume knob fell off when it was all the way up. They partied till dawn on cheap speed. I lost count of the times I woke up at three-thirty a.m. with them slam dancing on the floor over my head. If you rang their doorbell and asked them to stop they'd turn off the stereo for at least five minutes before you'd hear, *Spiderman,*

spiderman, does whatever a spider can... and the jackboots would start pounding the ceiling again. When you called the cops they never came.

I was lucky if I got three hours of sleep a night. Got where I was so exhausted all the time I almost lost my job. Couldn't focus or concentrate on anything, was always nervous and stressed out. After awhile I couldn't stand it anymore and I just snapped. I stole a piece of heavy equipment from a nearby construction site and drove it towards our building. After parking in front I maneuvered the crane so that the huge electro-magnet was hanging just outside the Tackle Box Faces' living room window. As I hit the juice the window erupted outwards as the TBFs flew through the air, yanked by their metal body jewelry which pulled their flesh out to thin cones. Once I had them all stuck wiggling on the electro-magnet like roaches on a gluestick, I put the crane into drive and started heading towards the beach. We'd see if those jangling tallywackers could float.

crack

One weekend Dave took me down to LA to visit some of his old haunts. On Saturday afternoon we were wandering through a blasted landscape in a particularly grim section of downtown. The seedy storefronts, alcoholic bars, and burned-out warehouses seemed to trigger some suppressed need in Dave. On a sudden impulse, he decided to buy some crack. Once he had made up his mind it seemed to take him less than five minutes to score. He almost seemed guided to the drug by some biological radar. As he stood there with the rock in his hand, I said, "Man, that stuff's going to kill you."

"No," Dave said. "Crack doesn't kill you. It does something that might even be worse. You want to know what crack does to you? I'll show you."

There was a greasy unshaven bum lying against a wall about fifty feet away. He was resting his head on an old backpack that was tattered and soiled. Dave walked up to him and said, "Hey, man, if you give me your backpack, your clothes, and your socks, I'll give you this rock of crack."

The homeless person instantly leapt to his feet. Within seconds he had stripped off all his clothes and his backpack and had piled them up in front of Dave. Dave handed him the crack. The homeless man walked off in nothing but his dirty tennis shoes, the white crystalline rock held up in his hand, in search of a pipe to smoke it with. Dave pointed to the pile of clothes to prove his point. We walked off and left them there.

some Party

I've been to New Age Hell and come back to tell tale of it. Long-haired vendors walking around through the crowd, holding up psilocybin caps, yelling, "Mushrooms! Mushrooms!" People smoking so much dope the skunky smell overpowers all the burning sage and incense, makes a great green cloud that rises up through the gorge to the sky. We're talking the biggest party this county has ever seen; we mean telemarketing, tour flight packages, the works. All the local folks just raking it in selling organic veggie burritos and alfalfa sprout salads for three bucks a pop, making money, making money, more than this town has seen in a long time.

And old Truck the party animal doing five hits of acid, blowing a million doobies on top of a steady bladder flow of beer, tripping his balls off, getting so sunburnt he almost glows in the dark. We're walking out, his mind fried by the enormity of what he's just seen, ten thousand people spilling out into the parking lot and suddenly Truck is everybody's friend. He sees two girls walking by with a cooler and says, "My, my, ladies, what are you up to?"

"We're doing all the work," one of them says. "The women do the work while the men stand around drinking vodka drinks."

Truck spots someone with a drink and yells out, "Sir, sir, let me have a hit of that vodka drink. It's my duty as a male."

Then he turns to the women and says, "Would you all mind if I sit on that cooler and you could just carry me on out of here?"

Well, the next morning he's hurting. So what does he do? Gets up and on an empty stomach drinks half a bottle of Jim Beam. He becomes real talkative and then we don't see him for awhile. Finally someone says, "Where's Truck?" I head down to the bathroom 'cause that's the last direction we'd seen him go. When I saw his shoe sticking out from underneath the stall door I knew things were bad. Truck was face down, melding with the porcelain bowl in a unity pact cemented by barf. Spent the rest of the day sacked out on the futon he'd set up next to his car.

When the sun set over the valley the air itself was so blue, then pools of red lit the clouds up purple and majestic. "That was some party," Truck announced from his futon. "My body feels like a used SOS pad."

Slacker High Noon

My name's Sammy Chill and for a couple of years now I've enjoyed a reputation on the local coffeehouse scene as King of the Slackers. Anyone who knows me knows I'm always chillin'. My entire wardrobe cost less than thirty dollars and eighty percent of it I got for free from dumpster dives and Salvation Army drop-off points. I've worked hard at staying unemployed, scamming SSI, disability, food stamps, and anything else I can get my hands on. If I'm not squatting then I'm on a rent strike. Won't go to a show unless they put me on the list. Only drink from a free keg. And with no job to get in the way there's plenty of time to look for these things. Soup kitchen? I'm there. And you won't hear any complaints about the chef.

The only thing I'm a snob about is coffee. Caffeine is my scene. Most days I waste away in the local cafes rising a steady escalator of java. I am an expert on the entire spectrum of the bean. I read poetry. Sometimes you'll even see me with a copy of *Being And Nothingness* in my hands, not necessarily reading but trying to look like I understand it. It's a tough life getting nothing done.

But then word hit the scene that I had a rival. A guy named Slow Charlie. Someone even more lax who was calling himself King of the Slackers. Stealing the title I had loafed so hard to earn. I was outraged! Well, actually I was only mildly upset. Come to think of it, I didn't really care at all. But I knew that one day we'd meet and there would be a showdown which only one of us would walk away from. He who walked away would be the loser because the winner would be too kicked back and relaxed to move. We'd see who could put their feet highest on the table.

I never went out and looked for this guy but as fate and the general incestuous nature of coffeehouses would have it we ran into each other at the Sacred Grounds Cafe. As soon as I saw Slow Charlie I knew I was in trouble. To begin with, he was overweight. Not naturally fat, it wasn't genetic obesity. No, he had that obvious out of shape couch potato flab which didn't match his body proportions and could only originate in long bouts of inactivity. We made eye contact, recognized each other, and he came over and sat down at my table.

"I've heard a lot about you."

"And I about you."

Then we both launched into it, a comparison of who was more lazy, more slack. We compared our extensive travels through the welfare system and low-to-no-rent housing. Our avoidance of even part-time jobs. Our lack of protestant work ethic, aspirations, consumer clout, yuppie inclinations or future goals. Sure, the two of us tried to look passive and nonchalant but you could tell our hearts were in it. I was drinking the house special, a Delta Mud Cappuccino which actually had a layer of ground coffee beans on the bottom. Trying to press my advantage I asked for a beverage comparison.

"That's easy," my opponent said. "I'm drinking a quadruple espresso."

"But there's a head of white foam three inches deep in your cup," I protested.

"Fifty percent of it's half-and-half. The rest is pure cream."

Jesus, I'm thinking, half of what he's drinking is clogging his veins and the other half's constricting them. He'd definitely taken the lead with that one. I regained some ground when he found out I was still living with my parents and his had kicked him out three months before. But they still wrote him checks.

He tried to start talking about the medication he was on but I changed the subject quick. Didn't want to be there all night. Our duel went on as we compared our ability to drop out of colleges and never hold a job for over two months. We slacked neck and neck to prove who was the laziest. By the end we were both lying on the cafe floor half asleep. That's when he pulled his coup de grace.

"What book are you reading?" I asked.

"A biography of Jackie Collins," Slow Charlie said.

"Sounds like pretty easy reading," I sneered.

"It is. I've read it fifteen times."

"Why so often?" I asked.

"I've got a really bad memory," he replied.

That's when I realized I'd lost my crown. I rolled over to shake his hand, but even through all the caffeine the new king had managed to fall fast asleep.

trust

One day while Devon was walking around the neighborhood he came upon an old 1965 Buick LeSabre that had the keys in the ignition. It was a monstrous boat of a car, with a 450 engine and an old-fashioned back seat which was actually big enough for two people to make love in. Devon was zipping on speed at the time and saw the vehicle as a logical way for him to go faster. The doors were unlocked, so he got in and took off. For the next forty-eight hours he drove the car nonstop, snorting lines of crank off the dashboard and washing them down with straight shots of whiskey. It was a grand old car from the glory days of travel, before we knew how destructive such machines were to the environment and ozone. Devon relished in the faded luxury of the tattered vinyl seats. He loved punching it until the speedometer needle rose up to one hundred and ten. Not like one of those wimpy little imports that only register up to eighty miles per hour. Devon swerved it around the LA roads in a hyperactive delirium, pulling over at times to pick up loose high school girls, seducing them with crank and alcohol, stealing their cherries on the back seat and then rudely dumping them out on a street corner miles away from their homes. Let them spend the quarter to explain their woes and problems to Mommy and Daddy, he had to keep moving.

After putting almost four hundred miles on the car Devon brought it back to the same parking space where he had originally found it. He left the keys in the ignition, the doors unlocked, and went home to the squat to crash. When Devon passed by the same place a few days later the car was still there and the keys were still in the ignition. He thought it might be an abandoned vehicle but when he checked the odometer he saw that someone had added about twenty-five miles since he had used it. The doors were still unlocked. So Devon got in and drove to the grocery store to pick up a few cases of generic beer.

For the entire four months Devon lived in the area he used the car on a regular basis. The Buick was always parked in the same place and the keys were always there. Sometimes when he went by, the car was gone and he realized that the real owner must be using it. He didn't mind though. The real owner used it much less than he did. They must have known Devon was driving their car because he often left telltale signs such as cans of beer or half-smoked roaches sitting on the front seat. But they didn't seem to care. The car always ended up in the same parking space with the keys in the ignition and the doors unlocked. So Devon tried to repay the favor by always returning the Buick to the same place, too. He never bothered to make up a separate set of keys because the whole relationship was based on trust. The last time Devon borrowed the car he gave it a wax job, a full tank of gas, and left a little note scotchtaped to the steering wheel which just said *Thanks*.

Raving Lunatic

It was in the Leidseplein, a touristy area of Amsterdam, that we ran into the raving lunatic. He was a heavy-browed sullen little man who held out his hand and asked us something in Dutch. We shrugged our shoulders to show we didn't understand. He proceeded to follow us down the street, asking in German, French, and finally English.

"Can you spare any change?" he demanded petulantly. I just walked away, ignoring him completely.

"I'm sorry," Julia said. "We already spent all our money in the bars."

The man flew into a rage. "I didn't ask the woman," he screamed. "I asked the man. What kind of man lets his wife speak for him? Of course you have money! You're fucking Americans, all Americans have money! And they do not share it with the rest of the world!"

We walked away quickly. Luckily the raving guy didn't follow, but he kept screaming at us, ever more foully and at the top of his lungs, until we rounded the end of the block.

"Can you believe that guy?" Julia commented. "Anybody who's fluent in five languages is smart enough to get a job. I'll bet you he's panhandled in all the cities of Europe, going from place to place sponging off people, an international bum."

"Maybe he works as a translator for all the panhandlers in front of the United Nations in New York," I suggested.

Later that night we saw the raving man again. By this time his anger had boiled over to the point where he no longer needed a human host or receiver. His hateful screaming diatribe was frightful to witness, a nonstop stream of profanities and degrading comparisons. I couldn't imagine what horrible depravity had brought him to this condition. No one stood within a hundred feet of him. He was all alone in the dark swirling mists, screaming at a lamp post.

Eddie Blue

Eddie Blue was a professional substance abuser. He was roommates with my dealer, the Stone Dog. That was back when Dog was selling thorazine. I mainly went to him for the staples like pot and mushrooms but the whole thorazine thing had kind of come out of left field. Along with stoners and trippers, Dog had built up a steady clientele of people into downers. But when his main source who worked at a pharmacy got busted Dog had to turn to a motley crew of pill heads to keep him in reds and valiums. One day he bought two thousand tablets of thorazine from a punk rocker who was scamming SSI. The punk had managed to convince the state that he was crazy and got six hundred dollars and a full bottle of thorazine every month. He never did the pills and when he had accumulated almost five years' worth, he sold the bulk to Dog for a tidy little sum. Hey, that punk wasn't crazy. Dog sold them to his regular downer crew claiming they were just as good as valiums. They didn't seem to notice the difference. Even the stoners and acid heads ended up taking quite a few.

Thorazine basically separates your brain from your central nervous system. Under its influence motor reactions get all out of whack. It's like you can feel gaps opening up between your neuro-transmitters so the signals and sparks can't leap across. Words slur and puddle. Conversations seem to be crawling through thick mud. Parties at Dog's place became agglomerations of Couch Potatoes. I only did thorazine once or twice because the drug can make permanent changes in your brain. But none of the other druggies seemed to care. During the Super Bowl I saw Eddie Blue eat ten tablets at one time. For someone who ate a lot of thorazine Eddie still managed to remain completely crazy.

Living in the same apartment as the Stone Dog could keep one in a constant state of inebriation just on the scraps and leftovers. Only Eddie felt he needed to do exponentially more drugs than everyone around him. This was not a matter of machismo but honest desire on Eddie's part. I don't think the phrase, "That's enough," existed in his vocabulary.

One night we were at a warehouse party South of Market. It was four in the morning and we had all been drinking and smoking since three that afternoon. Eddie met some guy who had doses. He had never seen the dealer before but the guy insisted his blotters were strong and that Eddie shouldn't eat more than one. We all bought a couple and decided to trip the next night when we had recovered from that day's drinking. That wasn't good enough for Eddie. He bought four hits and ate them right then and there. He didn't even start to get off until the sun was coming up.

Eddie's room was the size of a shoebox but he had given over more than half of it to a pot growing operation. This started out as a large wooden box filled with fluorescent lights which he nailed to one wall. Yet as the plants grew in number and size he was forced to expand. The growing operation took over two-thirds of the room and his whole closet. When they went into the budding stage he knocked out one of his bedroom walls to make more space for lights. By the time harvest rolled around Eddie had been forced out of his room completely and slept on the couch in the living room. As I went to visit the Dog I could smell his crop from almost two blocks away.

Eddie was notorious for doing little domestic things which were annoying even to people as far gone as his roommates. At one point he became obsessed with the idea that someone was stealing his milk.

"Now, we were stealing his milk," Dog readily admitted to me. "But no more than in the average household." Of greater importance than the lost milk itself was identifying the culprit. Eddie came up with a novel test of guilt. He threw five hits of acid into the half-gallon in the refrigerator and waited for the thief to show himself. "That was a real drag," Dog told me. "I get up for work all hung over from drinking the night before. Eat a bowl of cereal on my way out the door. Two hours later I'm at work and the boxes I'm hauling start talking back to me. That's when I realized my corn flakes must have been electric."

The apartment they lived in could have made a garbage dump look clean by comparison. We called the place the Dog House. Every surface was covered with old beer cans, overflowing ashtrays, and the styrofoam refuse of greasy burgers and fries. Dirty bongs were crusted with geologic layers of resin. The place was so full of trash that the huge population of roaches rarely even made it to the top of the piles. Only guys had lived in those rooms for over five years so the walls and carpets had absorbed a rotted testosterone stench reminiscent of the Lost Jock Strap. In the living room the carpet had absorbed so many stains of spilled beer and bongwater that the rug looked more like a camouflage pattern than its original eggshell blue. We used to make jokes that if it got any dirtier even the vermin would move out.

The maintenance problem was just one of many reasons why they all got evicted that spring. Their landlord also cited "the constant flow of surly looking characters" going in and out of the place. It didn't help that they had a habit of throwing huge parties every weekend which usually had at least three hundred people in attendance and a rock band. Their parties had been shut down so many times that Dog had gotten to know all the local beat cops on a first name basis. Though they didn't find out till later, the real reason the landlord wanted them evicted was because he was trying to sell the building to some foreign investors and he wanted to convince them it was a prime piece of real estate.

When the word came down, everyone but Eddie went out and found a new place to live. For some reason it didn't seem to register on Eddie's one remaining neuron that he really had to leave. He spent that last month partying while Dog and the others sobered up enough to sign new leases. In fact, Eddie spent the last four days there on a frightening LSD and whiskey binge. After sixty-two hours without sleep Eddie passed out on the front porch. Dog and the others found it was impossible to wake him, but he was still breathing so his condition couldn't have been that bad. It was a real bitch though having to keep stepping over him as they moved their stuff out. Eddie just slept through all the packing, clanking, and hoisting of furniture.

The morning of the first of the month was bright and sunny. Behind Eddie's comatose form on the porch the apartment was empty. Only the sleeper's belongings remained. The sound of birds singing woke Eddie up. He stood up, stretched in the sunlight, and said, "Today is going to be a great day!" But he had stood up too fast. All the sick alcohol-depleted blood ran to his head. Eddie passed out, fell down two flights of stairs, and finally came to rest on a lower landing where his tortured stomach purged itself in a huge puddle of green bile. The vomit pooled around Eddie's unconscious head, soaking into his hair and ear. Meanwhile, at the bottom of the stairs, the landlord was leading two well-dressed foreign businessmen up to the apartment. The landlord was really talking the place up. With each step he extolled the magnificent virtues of the little piece of the American Dream they were about to buy.

cheap Motel

Paula began going out with some guy named Lenny she met in the parking lot after a Grateful Dead show. He had been living in his car for the past two years. Less than a week after the two met they had taken up residence on the couch in our living room. Now me and my roommates recognized Lenny for what he was - a homeless person - but Paula insisted that he "just had a few problems which needed sorting out." She claimed he was really a nice guy, people just misunderstood his free spirit. We weren't buying it and laid down the ultimatum that she either kick Lenny out or leave with him. She chose to go.

We expected to see her back in a couple days but she was tenacious. Paula camped out with him in that cramped car through two weeks of winter rains. Lenny, of course, was used to it and didn't mind at all, he was just glad for the company, but Paula came from a nice family back east. She was used to clean towels and wall-to-wall carpets. When Thanksgiving rolled around the exposure finally broke her. She told Lenny they had to rent a hotel room for the holiday. At least for one night, she wanted to be indoors. Neither of them had much money but they had heard through the grapevine that you could get a cheap room for the night down by the MacArthur BART station in Oakland. Paula was new to the area, thus giving her the right to claim ignorance, and Lenny had no excuse whatsoever, but you'd think one of them would have thought twice when it looked like they were driving into the set of *Boyz In The Hood*.

After they checked into a cheap motel Paula took off all her clothes and climbed into bed, luxuriating in the purr of the magic fingers massage. Lenny went out to get them something to eat. He was walking in the door with their Thanksgiving dinner from Kentucky Fried Chicken when two big guys wearing backwards baseball caps followed him in. Paula started screaming. They pulled out huge guns and she shut up quick. "Narcotics," the two gangbangers said in unison. "Give us your narcotics. We know you have some."

"Aw, man," Lenny said. "All we got's a couple joints' worth."

"Give it to them!" screamed Paula.

After he handed over the pot one of the intruders said, "Okay, now give us all your money."

Lenny fished over their last twenty bucks.

And the two of them walked out of the room. They didn't even bother closing the door. After leaving, the robbers walked upstairs to the motel room directly above Lenny and Paula's. A party had already been raging in there and when the two guys entered with fresh money and drugs it got even louder. Lenny and Paula's twenty bucks was soon translated into a crack run. Beneath the party Lenny and Paula were trembling in its noise. Twenty minutes passed before they were brave enough to even get up and close the front door. Then it took another hour to raise the courage to call the cops. Only the phone was dead. The party raged on and on, its crazed volume driving any thoughts of sleep or peace from the couple's minds. Later that night Lenny snuck down to the front office to try and call the cops from the manager's desk. The manager just laughed at his pathetic attempt. "Don't you understand, boy?" the old guy said. "Gang's took over the whole motel. They shut down the phones and everything. And seein' how much ah that rock they smokin' I can guarantee you they ain't leavin' before tomorrow afternoon."

So Lenny and Paula spent a sleepless night huddled in a shivering silent bed, staring in terror towards their noisy ceiling, waiting for the gunmen to return. They didn't dare risk a dash to their car until the gang finally left the next evening around five. The couple drove straight to the nearest police station. After telling their whole story, the first thing the officer filing the report asked them was, "What the hell were you doing down there in the first place?" Two days later Paula had her parents wire her money and she flew back home. Lenny was recently spotted looking for a miracle ticket in the parking lot of a Kentucky Fried Chicken.

Grave Robber

Jimmy just couldn't stay out of bone yards. He loved the look and feel of the granite headstones, the bars on the crypts so like the tattooed prison bars he flaunted. He developed a hobby of going grave walking late at night with his friend Freddy Kruger. Freddy's last name was really Jones but we called him that because he had a big burn on his face and nobody liked him. Sometimes these two would steal the heads off of cemetery idols and perform weird rituals with them while they were on PCP. One of these ceremonies set his bedroom on fire and got Jimmy kicked out of the Pink House squat. But him and Freddy kept that shit up anyway.

One night they noticed the door to a mausoleum was open so they went on in and broke into the vaults quite easily. Somewhere back in the darkness and cobwebbed marble they pulled open a coffin which contained a hundred-year-old baby. Even though it was swathed in bandages they knew it was a valuable find, and without a second's thought, carried the dead baby away with them.

When I talked to Jimmy about the incident later he tried to belittle the morbid intents of their expedition. "It wasn't no big thing," he said. "Me and Freddy were just poking around in there searching for skulls for our bone collection. I looked into one of the coffins, saw a nice specimen and grabbed it. How was I to know the rest of the body would come along with it?"

Jimmy Tar was living in his van at the time of the grave robbing, but for some reason he brought the dead baby mummy to Bleak House. When he walked into the living room all the punk rock kids were drinking beers and doing bong hits. Jimmy just carried his bundle in past them and went through the house back to the kitchen table. He cleared off the old tuna fish cans, wilted lettuce leaves, beer bottles, soggy twinkies, and dirty plates, and set the baby down. As people began to filter in he got a butcher knife out of the dish rack and cut open the bandages over the baby's face. They stripped away dry and rotted as old banana peels. Then once he got underneath all the wrappings the baby's face stared up at them. It looked like a Barbie doll head which had been left out in the sun too long until it had come to resemble some kind of grotesque raisin more than a human being. Slowly it began to seep in through all the stoned roommates minds. 'Holy shit, what the hell is he doing?' 'He's putting that dead thing down right on top of the place we eat our food on.' 'I wonder if there's worms in it?' 'He's crossed the line.'

Finally Louella just lost it. "Get that the fuck out of here, Jimmy!" she screamed. "I don't know what kind of fucking weird gross-out trip you're on, but you can't bring it in here! Next time for all we know you'll bring in a live one. You're a freak! A psycho! Get out!"

At that point Sean panicked and called the cops. Jimmy cuddled up his mummified baby as gently as if it were a living one and ran out the door into the night.

The cops spotted Jimmy on the street and chased him into a busy nightclub called The Pit. Jimmy managed to move swiftly through the crowd by telling people it was a sick baby he had to get to the hospital. He left the mummy by the back door and escaped into the night alleys of Oakland.

The police are still looking for Jimmy Tar. He's a fugitive, wanted for violation of a corpse and a list of other crimes that highlight the law's macabre descriptiveness. Sam Dangerous said the residents of Bleak House broke the cardinal rule by telling the cops they knew anything when the officers came by asking questions. But what did they really tell them? What did they know? That Jimmy was crazy? Everyone knew that. They found Jimmy's van abandoned in the parking lot of a Safeway near Berkeley. Beyond that, everything about him is an unknown.

Every now and then I get phone calls from Jimmy Tar. He's always someplace far away, calling long distance from a pay phone. His general mood is one of total paranoia. Jimmy always asks me how close the cops are to him but he refuses to tell me where he is. He doesn't like being on the run. Last time I talked to him he said he wishes he could just settle down, and maybe start a family, you know, have kids even.

The Tales of G. Spot Fitzgerald

I was tired as shit after staying up all night fucking Carrie. That girl gets off work around three a. m., randy as a raccoon, and most nights I end up screwing till around dawn. Then about six or six-thirty I go back to sleep for an hour or two, and have to be up and at work by nine.

I work for a weekly paper and am in charge of the singles section. I'm the Swami of Sex, the Meister of Love. My job is to hook the perverts up with each other like a social connect-the-dots, and I never stand back far enough to see what it all looks like because I'm too busy in what I'm doing right here and now. And that's getting people laid, including yours truly. My job is to wade through poontang and sperm deep as a river of clorox and make sure people's life rafts tie up together. They say the sexual revolution's dead, but I plan on kicking it a few times before it's gone. The name of the game is Love, or more importantly, Sex, and if I create a hundred successful dates not only do I make a commission there's even enough sloppy seconds left over for me to get my own willy wet, too. But that seems to be part of my problem. You see, I got more than seconds, I've even got thirds. These days I'm seeing three women at once and it's getting a little out of hand. But your boy Bobby Zone is just having such a good time he doesn't want it to stop. Me and my little penis, who I affectionately call G. Spot Fitzgerald, have never had a workout like this before and we're gonna go with it as long as it goes. Sure, it'll all end in disaster, but what a crash.

I just can't decide which of these women I like better: Carrie, who isn't that much to look at, but she's just such a little fuck machine; or Lorraine whose sex drive isn't as strong as I'd like it to be, but Jesus, what a bod. And those tits! Big as NBA regulation basketballs. It's like being a baby again. And then there's Moria, a spaced-out little goth chick who's fresh on my radar screen. I don't even know where she's coming from. But, ooh, when she parades around my bedroom with those rings in her pussy lips and all that black death rocker lingerie, I just can't control myself. I'm getting it from both ends these days.

But you know how women are. They'll only give it up for a little while before they want you to make up your mind about things. And now all these girls are starting to give me friction. Getting into that deadly talk about commitments and other depressing matters. But none of them's worse than Carrie. It's like the girl wants me to marry her or something! We've only been seeing each other for nine months, fer chrissakes! I keep explaining to the girl that our relationship is purely sexual, nothing more. But that only shuts her up for a couple of days before she starts throwing crying fits, going, "Don't you love me?" and "I'm just an object to you," and all that other girlie-girl talk. So I just threaten to break up with her and that shuts her trap real fast. And next thing you know, after one of those tense emotional conversations we're rolling around the bed again fucking like chipmunks. Then she goes off to her night job, and I make a date with Lorraine and we go out to some hippie place or across the bridge to the redwoods to fool around in the back of her VW van, or I go out with Moria to some speed metal club that fries our eardrums before she takes me back to her black-painted room with all the melted candles and the Slayer posters on the walls and she does all kinds of kinky stuff like fucking me up the butt with a black leather dildo, and I crawl back home half-drunk around two a.m., get about an hour's sleep before Carrie wakes me up and we fuck till dawn and then I'm back to work again.

And work's another freak show. I couldn't ask for a better job. All day long people call in their sexual fantasies to me and I listen to them, condense them into paragraph form, and type them up. Every issue of our paper has about five or six pages of singles ads and I write almost all of them. And talk about weird! I talk to some real freaks at my job. The phone will ring. I'll pick it up and there'll be some gruff voice on the other end that sounds like it belongs to a pot-bellied businessman. But he'll say something like, "Post-op transsexual seeks hairy man in his sixties to play Daddy with. I'll be the daughter you never had."

Or it'll be something like, "Skinhead god seeks water pipe queen for nude motorcycle ride to LA."

Or, "Are coffee enemas your idea of a hot breakfast date? If so, contact the Queen of Spew. Rubber garments required. Please, no freaks or sickos."

Or, "Black-clad fan of the Marquis de Sade seeks pale pasty queer boy to talk about machines and computers with. Give me your address and we'll interface."

It's like that all day long, nonstop. Enough to drive you crazy. Some days I have to sneak out and jerk off in the men's room three times in one shift. I can't help but make crude jokes about pussy farts and sphincters all day long. Some of the women in the office think I'm a misogynist, but fuck 'em. If I hated women why would I be sleeping with three of them?

I drink about a pot and a half of coffee every day at work. That's what it takes to get me through. Off the job I use more exotic stimulants, coke or speed usually. One of these days I'll be able to eliminate sleep completely. It's just a waste of time.

Well, finally five-thirty rolled around and not a minute too soon. I put the finishing touches on my last singles ad. It was a real winner, *Turd boy seeks turd girl. No smooth poopers.* And I got the fuck out of there.

I needed to take a nap before I went out that night. I had a coffee date with Lorraine, and later a club date with Moria, and then always at the crack of dawn there was the crack of Carrie. But when I got home I knew I was in deep shit. There, sitting in my bedroom, were both Moria and Lorraine. And not only that, Carrie's best friend was there with them. All of them began screaming at me at once and it looked like the feeding frenzy from *Jaws 3.*

"I'm sorry, I'm sorry," I screamed. "I'm just a guy." After about a half hour their screaming calmed down and I apologized diligently and profusely.

"I'm sorry," I said. "I just wanted to make you all happy." Lorraine and Moria thought this was sweet, but of course, all along my main intention hadn't been making *them* happy. I broke out some coke and some beers and soon the talk got a lot more civil. But Carrie's best friend wasn't buying any of it.

"How can you listen to this lying sack of shit?" she yelled. "I've never seen a bigger creep in my life."

"Aww, I'm not that bad," I said, flashing that cute smile of mine that always works like a charm. "In fact I'm kind of lovable."

Lorraine and Moria instantly agreed because I could tell that they had enough coke and alcohol in them that they were getting to that I-want-to-fool-around state of things, but Carrie's best friend wouldn't take the bait. It was around this time that I suggested we have a menage-a-trois. Moria, kinky little slut that she is, was into it but Lorraine was real skeptical and kept shaking her head no. But both me and Moria got to work on her and about two drinks later we managed to convince her that it was worth a try. We began feeling each other up and taking our clothes off. Carrie's best friend shot up from her chair, fuming. "I can't believe you all," she shrieked.

"What?" I said, genuinely surprised. "It's all in good fun."

"But what about Carrie?" she said.

"What about her?" I replied. "She's not here."

"Don't you care about her feelings at all?"

"You're welcome to join in if you want to," I suggested.

Carrie's best friend just screamed and stomped out. The front door slammed as she left the apartment.

By that time I wasn't even paying attention. Two women at once. Every man's dream. It had been so long since I'd slept that my dreams were leaking out and becoming reality. People talk about the joys the poets sing of and heaven on earth but let me tell you, after that night - well, my life has known no greater pleasure. The last thing I remember was Moria and Lorraine helping each other get dressed to go and Lorraine said to Moria, "You know, I always thought I might be a lesbian." And then I dropped down into a black, bottomless sleep. An abyss. It was like drifting in the darkest part of outer space.

I was woken by exploding stars. Light burst over me, things shattered all around me, there was a roaring like a thousand bees. Carrie stood above me, screaming at the top of her lungs and throwing glasses, vases, cassette tapes, and any other object she could find at me. I tried to shake the drunken drowsy sleep from my eyes but it was like rising up through a quagmire. "You bastard," she squealed. "You back-stabbing little shit. Goddamn you!"

"What are you so upset about?" I moaned. "What's wrong?"

She just let out a gurgling whine of pure frustration and kept throwing things at me. I sat up in the bed and realized there was dirt all over me. In the sheets, in my hair. In her fury, Carrie had thrown my potted plants at me. As I tried to stand the dirt rained down off me like a dead man crawling out of a grave. Carrie only got angrier and angrier. "I just can't believe you," she screamed. "Sometimes I think the only eyes you have is the one on the end of your dick!"

I swear to God, you try to make women happy and this is the thanks you get. Sometimes I think the only tales little G. Spot Fitzgerald writes are sob stories.

work Is Hell

My introduction to the world of work and toil came early, when I was only fifteen-and-a-half, six months younger than the legal working age. I got my job with a special labor permit supplied by my employer. They had a long explanation that claimed it was all on the up and up, but I suspect my job was completely off the books. Even though I was an under-the-table guy, they still took taxes out of my check and that money probably never made it to Uncle Sam. If anything, it went to buy my supervisor a new bag of dope. My assignment was to do contractor work in a gigantic nylon processing factory. Contractor work, for those of you unfamiliar with the business, usually means janitorial needs of the lowest and most filthy kind. We got the jobs too gross and disgusting for the factory's union labor to dirty their hands with. For minimum wage (three dollars an hour, at that time) we scraped gelatinous gunk out of air conditioner vents, cleaned sewage drains, and mopped up spills of dangerous chemicals, while the fifteen-dollar-an-hour guys stood around and laughed at us.

A job like ours didn't bring in the bold and brightest minds. No. My work crew was composed of sixteen-year-old pot-smoking dirtballs, high school dropouts, and psycho

Vietnam vets. In short, we were people who couldn't find a job anyplace else. Because of their age, the Vietnam vets were usually appointed as supervisors, even though these guys had IQs around 70, and 65 points of that were focused on constant LSD and Viet Cong flashbacks. While not the greatest leaders, these guys were experts at sneaking liquor and drugs into the factory and they could still mop a floor under the influence of three quaaludes. Many were the times that, under their tutelage, cleanup jobs in the industrial recesses of the factory degenerated into whiskey-drinking, joint-toking parties that left a bigger litter of beer cans than the mess we were supposed to eliminate in the first place.

When I was fifteen-and-a-half I didn't really understand what work was. Most of my chores up to that time were mere housework for which I garnered a paltry allowance, which wasn't keeping up with the sophisticated needs of a teenager. It took me more than two weeks to save up enough money to buy the new Styx album. I needed a bigger influx of cash. So when my friend Bud Wood said the contractor agency he worked for had a couple of openings I leapt at the opportunity. In my mind I saw a nirvana of easy cash, I might even make enough money to buy a car. Until then my concepts of work had come mainly from movies and TV; that and my father's constant lectures on the terrors of the real world. I had seen Charlie Chaplin's *Modern Times* and thought work must be like those factory scenes, hard and physical, but with constant moments of comedy. I took the film to be a parody, and thought a job couldn't really be that bad. I had no concept of the constant crushing boredom that is the worst aspect of any task.

My first day on the job I reported in wearing only jeans and a t-shirt. After a short briefing in the cafeteria we were given safety glasses and ear plugs, and our crew descended into the depths of the factory. The further we went into the assembly lines the hotter it got. We passed row upon row of screaming machines spinning nylon thread onto huge cardboard rolls. After walking for a half-hour we ascended some stairs to the floor above the rows of spinning machines. This was a great cavernous place filled with red hot pipes and valves belching steam at odd intervals. On this level the raw nylon which came in gigantic blocks was melted into a liquid and pumped through the pipes at high pressures. The molten nylon was pumped through a valve perforated with hundreds of holes like a showerhead, and the liquid separated and solidified into strands of thread which went down through the floor to the spinning machines below. In order not to interrupt the manufacturing process, the room we now stood in had to be kept at a constant temperature of one hundred and twenty degrees. Our job: to climb onto the pipes and clean them off.

We were given bundles of rags and bottles of spray cleaner. So that we didn't burn our arms while climbing the hot pipes we were given long-sleeved wool shirts and insulated gloves. Now we were sweating bad enough because of the one hundred and twenty degree heat, but after being forced to wear the equivalent of a wool sweatshirt and gloves in those temperatures you can imagine the amount of liquid flowing out of us. You would think that under these conditions we would work quite slowly, and such would have been the case were it not for one thing. The pipes were so hot that when we sprayed the cleaner onto them it instantly began to boil and completely evaporated in less than five seconds. So if we wanted to do any cleaning at all we had to scrub the pipes with a rag as fast as humanly possible. In order to get anything done we had to wipe those pipes so frantically it gave us all arm cramps in less than three minutes. When we asked the supervisor how long we'd be on this job he said, "Until the whole floor is done."

This room of the factory was as big as four football fields lined up together. The place was damn near large enough to fly a plane through, and was filled from floor to ceiling with thousands upon thousands of red hot pipes. It would take over six months worth of eight hour days to clean them all. Not only that, but the machines created such a frightful noise you couldn't hear what your co-worker was saying even if he was screaming in your ear. To protect our hearing from damage we wore hard rubber ear plugs which soon had our ears throbbing with pain. Each of us must have sweat near to a gallon before the supervisor even finished explaining the job.

I remember walking up to clean my first pipe. I sprayed on the cleaner and it instantly evaporated into a vapor that fogged over my safety glasses till I could not see. My God, I thought, the reality of work is much worse than the Chaplin film.

Somehow I stuck it out through that first forty hour week. I was going to high school and then working every night till midnight. The combination of heat, school, and toil left me a walking zombie. My first paycheck brought in enough money to buy a complete collection of Styx albums but I had no time to listen to them. Everyone else in my work crew was suffering from a similar fatigue. Working for eight hours in one hundred and twenty degree heat drains all the mind, blood, and energy out of a person. We would have quit, only we needed the money too badly. I'd been getting bored with high school and had considered dropping out but I figured if this was what the work-a-day world was all about I'd have to find a way to stay in high school for the rest of my life. After about six hours on the job everyone in my crew would reach a mental state so blank and battered it approximated the trance one achieves after six hours of straight tequila shots. Even at that age of over-active hormones, I often found my fantasies in the boredom, noise, and heat switching from visions of naked women to images of an ice cold glass of Coca-Cola.

After three weeks in the inferno, Russell Stone, a pothead high school dropout who was our supervisor for the day, lost his cool and declared that the working conditions were intolerable, inhuman, and something had to be done about them.

"There isn't a worse job in America!" he screamed. "It's just not fair. We aren't a bunch of coolies."

"In this heat I don't think anybody could call us coolies," said Bobby Ray.

"What do you plan to do about it, Russell?" I asked while massaging the charley horse in my right arm.

Even though Russell was no structural engineer, he had been examining the machines we were working among and had noticed a number of air conditioning ducts which went through the room from the ceiling to the floor. These ducts were cool to the touch and though there were no vents in them diverting cool air into this room, they did have a number of sealed doors which could be opened with a little work. Russell got a screwdriver and wrench from the supply locker and a short while later succeeded in opening about twenty or thirty of the doors. Huge billows of cold air spilled out. In less than an hour the whole room cooled down about forty degrees to a tolerable eighty degrees Fahrenheit. We went back to work with gusto, delighted by the fact that the pipes were now cool enough to clean without the spray cleaner instantly evaporating.

Then a chorus of alarms, sirens, and flashing red lights went off. Instantly the floor was awash with high level supervisors from plant management. They demanded to know who was in charge. Everyone, including Russell, denied they were the boss or had any authority. It turned out that those ducts were the coolant system for the entire assembly line. They cooled the liquid nylon into strands. When Russell opened the doors the whole system lost pressure and overheated. The molten nylon blobbed up and clogged the showerhead valves above the spinning machines. The entire assembly line had to be shut down, dozens of spinning machines were so clogged with solidified nylon they had to be replaced completely. Russell's little act of proletarian revolt cost the factory hundreds of thousands of dollars.

Russell works at the Tasty Freeze now. He spends each day moving stock around in one of their giant refrigerators. Every time I see him he complains about how cold his job is.

The Demise of the Sizzlin' Androids

"Back in the early '80s I played in this band called the Sizzlin' Androids," said the keyboard player. His name was Davey, but he preferred to go by his techno nickname, DV. "We did country western tunes, mostly covers of songs by people like Johnny Cash, Buck Owens, and Roy Clark. There was just me and another keyboard player named Willie, and we were using mainly Moog synthesizers and those early Casios which had that ultra cheesy sound. Even though our material was all these old traditional songs, really boring done-to-death stuff, we made the tunes completely different by playing them like techno pop. Our main influence was Gary Numan and we spiced up the arrangements with spacy leads and obnoxious noises. The Sizzlin' Androids did a great psychedelic version of *Ring of Fire.* But I don't know, those were crazy times back then, I was always on speed or acid, some kind of drug, staying up for a week at a time, and Willie, well, Willie just plain drank too much. Some nights he'd drink so heavily on stage it really affected his timing. A few shows were total disasters. We gigged around for a couple of years but never rose above the level of an opening act. Played a lot of parties, some open mikes, but never made it big. Probably because we were always so fucked up. Finally, enough was enough. I remember the straw that broke the camel's back.

"We were opening for a local country band at the Hotel Utah. I'd seen Willie drink heavily before but that night he pounded the sauce like he was searching for some new plateau of zen. He must have killed a whole bottle of Jack Daniels by the end of our set. It was one of our sloppiest shows ever and Willie's leads were all over the place. We sounded more like industrial music than country western. Of course, the club paid us in beer which only added insult to injury. By the time the headline act got off stage we were completely shit-faced.

"You reach a point where you know things have gone too far. That night the moment came around last call. Willie had been mumbling about one thing or another for the past half-hour. I wasn't really listening to him because I was so drunk and stoned and my ears were still ringing from the show. Then he grabs me by the shoulder suddenly and says, 'You don't think I can eat a glass? You don't think I'm tough enough? Watch this.' He grabbed a glass off the bar and began to chew on the rim. By the time it shattered with his first good bite the bartender was there. 'Okay, that's it,' he said. 'I've had my eye on you two for a while now and that's far enough. You all are out of here. Hey Fred! Eighty-six these guys.' Willie tried to put up a fight but the bouncer was twice his size. Before I knew it we were both out on the street. I've got to get Willie and all our equipment home safely, I thought to myself. That wasn't going to be easy because I was really drunk too. Too drunk to drive. I stood there on the sidewalk thinking it over for a second.

"When I turned around, Willie had found a flat tire lying against the building. He had picked it up and was now swinging it around in the air, his whole body rotating with the movement. Before my horrified eyes, one of the revolutions knocked off the mirror of a VW van. Then he let go of it. The tire sailed through the air and landed smack on the windshield of a Mercedes, shattering the glass. I ran over, grabbed Willie by his shirt and dragged him off down the sidewalk. 'My God,' I hissed at him. 'We've got to get out of here before the cops come.' Willie's stationwagon was parked halfway down the block. All of our instruments were loaded up in the back of it. My primary concern was to get those synthesizers home safely.

" 'Okay, Willie,' I said. 'Give me the keys.'

" 'No way,' he replied dogmatically. 'The stuff's in my car so I'm driving.'

"I argued with him for a couple of minutes but he wouldn't budge. Finally, I gave in and let him climb into the driver's seat. My fear was that the cops were going to show up any second to investigate his little tire episode and I wanted him out of the area. Now this action was not as foolhardy as it might sound. You see, Willie only lived two blocks from the Hotel Utah. What could happen in two blocks?

"Even though it was a short drive, it was a dangerous one because in order to get to Willie's house we had to drive right in front of the Hall of Justice, you know, the City Jail. The place always has tons of cops parked out front and every night Willie came home drunk he had to drive right past them. Things went okay for the first block, Willie's steering was a little erratic but not too bad. Then, as we were driving past the Hall of Justice, Willie panicked and decided to take a short cut through an alleyway. He cut a sharp turn in the middle of the road, tires squealing and laying rubber as he shot into the narrow street. This alleyway was only big enough for one car to go through at a time. As we were flying down it I saw a set of headlights coming right at us from the opposite direction. They didn't appear to be stopping.

" 'Stop! Stop! Willie, for God's sake, stop!' I screamed at the top of my lungs. He looked over at me all nonchalant, and said softly, 'Why? I've got the right of way,' and proceeded to push the accelerator to the floor. The oncoming set of headlights appeared to be doing the same thing. I curled up into a fetal position and began screaming. Right when it seemed inevitable that worlds would collide and we'd end up as a commercial against drunk driving, both vehicles jammed on their brakes with a hellish shrieking of steel-belted radials. After we lurched to a stop I opened my eyes. The two front bumpers were less than six inches away from each other.

"Willie jumped out of the car, ready to kick some ass. He was shaking his arms in the air as he yelled, 'Get the fuck out of my alleyway!' The other driver leapt out of his van in a rage equal to Willie's. The guy was six foot two with a build like Tony Atlas. He'd whipped out a long bladed knife and was slicing it through the air, just waiting for an excuse to start cutting. 'Goddamn it, Willie,' I screamed. 'Get the fuck back in the car!' But any hope for common sense had been extinguished five beers ago. Willie charged the guy. I closed my eyes again. When I didn't hear a death shriek after about thirty seconds I opened them. In the glare of the headlights Willie and the big guy were laughing and patting each other on the back. They were all smiles. It turned out that the guy was Willie's next door neighbor. The two were best friends! Had known each other for years. After talking and joking together for a couple of minutes the big guy walked over to the passenger side of the stationwagon. I rolled down the window. 'You shouldn't let him drive in this condition,' he scolded. 'What kind of friend are you?'

"The big guy backed his van out of the alley and Willie got back behind the steering wheel. I tried to persuade him once more to let me drive but he wouldn't hear of it. 'Nonsense,' he said. 'We're only a few feet from home.' It was true. What could happen in a hundred feet?

"Willie revved the engine and punched the gas pedal to the floor. We shot out of the alley like a bullet from a gun. The car zoomed right past Willie's house. Everything seemed a swerving chaos. This was back before the earthquake, when we had all kinds of off-ramps and on-ramps onto 101. Before I know it, we've shot up one of these entry roads and we're on the freeway. The stationwagon is sliding all over the place, horns are honking, cars slamming on their brakes. By this time I'm stone cold sober. You have to understand that back then I was living in someone's garage. I hardly worked and had no money. My only valuable worldly possessions were the synthesizers that were in the back of this car. Music was my life, my driving passion. If those keyboards were destroyed in an accident that would have been the end. It would have taken at least two years to save up enough money to buy new ones and start playing again. And besides that, my whole life was passing before my eyes.

" 'What the fuck are you doing!?' I yelled at Willie. 'We've got to get off this road. Where the hell are you going!?'

" 'Maybe we're going to LA,' shouted Willie with devil-may-care enthusiasm.

"I was tempted to grab the wheel but that probably would have just sent us over the rail. Instead, I begged and pleaded with him to please get off at the next exit. He just laughed at me. 'Whatsa matter?' he said, his voice a demonic slur. 'Don't you have any sense of adventure?' I knew I was doomed. But through some miracle provided by the gods of sobriety and compassion Willie decided to get off a couple exits down the road. We were all the way out at the top of Market Street but that was close enough for me. At least I was within ten miles of home. As the stationwagon pulled onto Market he slowed down to about ten miles an hour. I opened the car door and rolled out onto the asphalt. Got a few scrapes and bruises, but I managed to crawl over to the sidewalk before another car came along and hit me. And you know what? That fucker didn't even stop. Just drove away down Market Street as the speed of the car slammed my door shut. I was left standing there, panting in the crisp night air, watching my synthesizers ride off to the Great Keyboard Graveyard in the sky. The walk home was long and cold.

"The next day I went by Willie's and collected up my stuff for the last time. He had made it home without incident and all the equipment was fine. But I couldn't take any more. I told Willie he'd crossed the line and I was breaking up the band. He got a little upset, mainly because he couldn't remember anything that had happened, but he eventually came to accept my decision. So I guess that was the demise of the Sizzlin' Androids."

Road Trip

If we had known about the blizzards, the automobile accidents, and the relentless attacks of fascist pigs, venomous truckers, and white trash racists, we wouldn't even have attempted the trip, not for something so simple as a wedding. But Squiggy was an old hometown pal of ours, and besides, it's not every day someone marries a girl who works in the lingerie department at K-Mart. So I taped a new muffler onto the primer-mobile and we loaded the trunk with dirty laundry, mushrooms and dope, and headed north out of the city. In San Francisco it was the same temperature as always but that was Christmas week and we knew the climate would turn way polar by the time we reached our destination in Montana. By Humboldt, the car was passing dead reefer fields and gray grass shining under new frost. The heater pumped out a steady whine. Yogi and Taj huddled in their leather jackets, cords of steam unwinding from their mouths. Everyone in the car was bald. They call me the Sultan of Stone. We're skinheads.

Don't get me wrong. We're not into the Nazi thing. Hell, I'll sit down and get stoned with anybody: black, white or paisley, as long as the bud's nice and green I don't care what color you are. We just like to slam around a pit when the music's loud and fast. In San Francisco that's okay and nobody gives each other shit. But outside those city limits, in the real world, the locals got their own ways of doing things. And they don't like people to mess with 'em or even drive through their turf.

The primer-mobile needs a hellacious amount of tinkering, jury-rigging, crazy glue, and positive psychological reinforcement before it can even leave the garage. It's a '68 El Camino that I bought for five hundred bucks when it was pretty much totalled. I rebuilt the front end and engine, and I'm still flushing money into it like I got a case of green diarrhea. Buffed all the paint off and primered the body but never did get around to painting over the primer so now the whole car's encased in a crispy shell of rust. When I drive over sixty something usually explodes in black smoke, and believe me, I always drive over sixty. So I had my doubts about how the car would perform on the big haul up north and back. We had to stop and reattach the muffler with electrical tape before we even left the city limits.

The first cop we saw in Idaho pulled us over as soon as our car crossed the state line. He was writing out a ticket for someone else, giving them the third degree through the driver's window. We passed him real slow but as soon as he saw a car with three bald dudes in it drool started dripping from his fangs. I've never seen someone write so fast, he must've finished the ticket in shorthand. That cop jumped into his prowl-mobile and was after us, all flashing lights and WHEEEOOOoooo. When I click the turn signal, instead of a flashing rear light all I get is an electrical smell of burning wires and of course Piggy's right on our ass so I'm wondering how we're going to pull over without him hitting us. Fast-thinking Taj waves a right turn hand signal out the passenger side window and we crunch into the ice on the shoulder. The cop stops, slams his door, stomps up to our car putting on his mirrored shades for hard-assness even though it's an overcast day, and when I roll down my window he yells, "What was that white shit you threw out the window?"

"What?!" I say, not knowing what the hell he's talking about.

"Him! Him!" he points to Taj. "I saw him throwing a baggie of white powder out the passenger side."

We freaked. The three of us were paranoid 'cause we had just smoked a doobie and the interior still reeked a bit and we had a QP of Humboldt bud, a half sheet of acid, and an ounce of mushrooms stashed in the luggage, but no powders. All we needed was for him to start poking around.

"Honest, man, he was just signaling a right turn," I pleaded.

"Listen, boy. I saw him throw something white into that field back there and I'm going to go look for it till I find it and bust you goons for what you're worth."

Now it's the middle of winter in Idaho. It's been snowing intermittently since October and the state's all dead and bare. There's a half foot of snow and permafrost on everything. The entire landscape is white. And he's going to find a handful of white powder in this Siberian blizzard country? I'm thinking, sure, buddy, you gonna hold us here till the thaw?

Slowly it dawns on the officer how ridiculous this is and he changes the subject. He's noticed our leather jackets with the metal studs, iron crosses, and anarchy symbols on them and he connects the coats with our haircuts. The cop puts his hand on his gun and goes, "Hey, what group are you all with?"

"What? You mean, like a rock group?" I ask.

"No. Survivalists? White supremacists? Nazi right wingers? You three ain't with the Aryan Youth Brigade, are you?"

"No, we're college students," I reply bluntly. "We always dress like this."

He doesn't believe us and goes back to his car and does a CIA scan, an FBI check, and an APB watch on us. And I'm sitting there in the primer-mobile thinking how radio signals are shooting from his squad car into outer space, bouncing off communication satellites, being networked through thousands of computer systems across the country and through the halls of law and order up to the higher offices of the government just to check three shmucks like us out. We, who haven't done anything. Hell, all I got is parking tickets. I don't think I like the police being so organized or having that much equipment. It's amazing what they'll do just because you don't look right to them. Much to his dismay, the officer found out we hadn't done anything wrong and he had no choice but to let us go. Not one to miss a single chance for assholism though, the cop warned me, Taj, and Yogi that he wanted us out of his part of Idaho as fast as our butts could move.

"Don't worry," I said as we pulled away. "We won't break the speed limit."

Less than five miles down the road all the tread fell off one of our rear tires. We pulled into the first town we came to, a place named Spread Eagle, Idaho. In the center of Spread Eagle we found a tire store on Beaver Street. It was two days before Christmas, and Best Tires was having its Santa Sale. Inner tubes as stocking stuffers. In the front window hung some tires which had been spraypainted green to look like wreaths. Ma and Pa and the local plumber and priest walked around the aisles with steel-belted radials wrapped in red ribbons and bows. Then suddenly everyone came to a stop and stared out the front window to watch the skinheads trying to fix their tire get hassled by the local cop. He pulled up with the sirens and lights going even though the primer-mobile was up on a jack. When the cop got out, the first thing he said was, "You know, you all're in my town now." Why are these cops always so damn territorial?

"What brings you boys to Spread Eagle?" he demanded.

"You people were the closest place with a tire store," I replied.

This must have sounded really suspicious so he began

peering around the inside of our car with his flashlight. Now three people had been living in this cramped space for two days on the road without stopping (except for repairs, that is). The interior and seats were a madness of old McDonald's containers, empty Coke cans, cigarette butts, candy bar wrappers, dirty laundry, smelly socks, half-eaten fruit, and general filth. You can just imagine the stench. Kind of a commingling of locker room and garbage dumpster.

The cop's face went sour, and he said, "You know, we got laws about keeping your car clean in this state."

I'm thinking, who are you, my mother? He makes us clean the car right there, which was one of the most humiliating things I've ever done but we did have all that shit in the luggage. While we're cleaning, he's checking us out on his radio. A couple minutes later the cop runs back to the primer-mobile laughing, "Hee, hee, I just talked to the state boys down the road. Hell, they just got done talking to you boys a few minutes ago. You all checked out okay."

"I guess that means we'll be safe for driving through the rest of the state," asked Taj sarcastically.

"You trying to get smart with me, boy?" the cop snapped quick as an ignition.

"Shut up, Taj," hissed Yogi.

"I think we got us a real smarty pants with us here," the cop said with sinister smugness. "Yessiree Bob, a fuckin-A genius."

"Shut up, Taj," I said.

"I'm not saying anything," Taj protested.

"Shut up anyway," I replied.

"Yeah, I think we gonna have to take you three into the station and do some extra special checks on you," the cop said with a smirk.

"Shut up, Taj," Yogi sneered angrily.

"I'm not saying anything."

There's nothing to do in a white room. The blankness

renders everything inert. Even pacing seems ridiculous. But you have to do something. Locking a man up with that much tension and nothing to take it out on is cruel and unusual. But worst of all, I still had a hit of acid in my wallet which they had somehow missed in the shakedown.

The cops had gone through the wallet right in front of me. A hit of acid is small enough to escape notice but I had wrapped this one in a big piece of aluminum foil because I was afraid I'd lose it. The officers poured everything out on a table and began sifting through the pile. Luckily, my wallet was so clogged and stuffed with dozens of old addresses scribbled on scraps of paper, coupons, Bazooka Joe comics, faded snapshots, half-written poems and song lyrics, long forgotten notes about things I'd better not forget, pleas to call people whose numbers I had lost, bounced checks, old concert tickets, lottery numbers, guitar picks, bus schedules, IOUs, bank statements, doctors' cards, crumpled magazine articles, ideas for drawings, bird feathers, and pieces of magnifying glass, but no money, that the officers didn't even notice a very large piece of aluminum foil full of LSD. So they crammed it all back in and handed the wallet to me. Then they threw me in the white room.

Would they search me again? I had to get rid of that acid. I looked around the room. Bare white walls, bare white floor. Smooth. Seamless. No cracks. The ceiling was white and flat too but there was a grate in it like a ventilation duct. Behind the grid I could see machinery. A camera? Or was I just being paranoid? Had to get rid of that acid. But were they watching? Then I noticed a little crack in one of the walls, down near the floor. Well, it wasn't really a crack but just a place where the white paint had flaked off the wall a bit. I could stuff the blotter in behind the flake. But the camera! It was just a ventilation duct. Yet those machines behind the grate... What if they searched me again? I stared up at the camera and thought that if they were watching I'd look really guilty by looking up at it. Then in one fast impulsive movement I snatched the aluminum foil from my wallet, tore the acid out of it, stuffed the hit into the crack in the wall, and ran back to the one white chair in the room and sat there trying to look really innocent. I blew it. If they were watching they saw the whole thing. Besides, the blotter stuck out like a sore thumb. Only half of it fit behind the flake. As soon as the officers walked back in their eyes would instantly dart to it. In a room so blank and white that colored piece of paper was the only thing which stood out. What if that was the whole point of this room: to put you in a space so empty there was only one place to try and hide your drugs, and they'd be watching and catch you while you were trying to stuff them? And I'd fallen for it like an idiot! Now they'd walk in and see the hit and bust me and I'd go to jail for a million years, but if I put it back in my pocket that'd look even more guilty. God, I felt like Raskolnikov! I could always just eat the acid, but then I'd be tripping in jail around cops, what if they tortured me and beat me up? What if I started talking about the drugs in the car? Had they searched the car? Had they found the drugs? Had they found the drugs but weren't going to tell us they'd found them because they were trying to get us to confess? If I tripped in jail I'd go crazy. No, things were complicated enough without LSD.

I wouldn't eat the hit. But what to do? Finally I got up and ran over to the crack, pulled the acid out and put it back in my wallet, all the while looking over my shoulder with a sick expression at the ventilation duct which may or may not have been a camera. I had just sat back down in the chair when the officers entered again.

There were two of them: the reedy redneck with bad teeth who had arrested us, and some three hundred pound galoot whose gut rolled over his tight belt like the spillway on a dam. Fatso kept gnawing on a toothpick. Occasionally he'd just let it hang in the spit on his swollen inner tube lips. The thin cop was scrawny and nervous, he had that macho I-always-have-to-prove-myself behavior one sees in guys who suffer from Short Dick Syndrome. I couldn't believe the other guy even had the energy to get off the couch and drag himself to work everyday.

"Well, you and your friend Yogi check out okay," said the thin pig. "But we're going to have to hold on to your friend Taj till we can check him out more. His kind of attitude usually betrays a criminal mentality."

"How long?" I gasped. The fear was already rising in me. Squiggy's wedding was in less than two days, we didn't have time for these good ole boys to jerk us around. What if they managed to get something on Taj? A huge ominous shadow fell across my brain, in it lurked visions of lawyers, astronomical legal expenses, prison time, gut-wrenching phone calls to parents.

"I mean, the state cops already checked us out," I continued. "Their search only took about fifteen minutes. Why do you all have to do it again?"

"Well, boy," the thin cop said happily. "In a case like this we don't want to leave any stones unturned. Who knows? Your friend could have killed somebody somewhere along the way. It's our job to be thorough."

The fat cop just stood behind him smiling, chewing on that toothpick and not saying nothing.

"How long do you think the check will take?" I asked, trying not to let the anger I felt leak out into my voice.

"Well, he'll definitely be spending tonight in the lockup. Then we'll see. Depending on what we hear we may be able to let him go sometime tomorrow morning."

"But we're on our way to a wedding," I pleaded. "If he spends the night in here I don't know if we'll make it. I thought those law enforcement computers could run an identity check in just a few minutes."

The cop looked so proud of himself I could have punched in his rotten yellow teeth.

"Now don't you be telling the law what kind of a schedule

it should be on," he said. "The law moves at its own pace. Sure we got computers, and they can run an ID check quick as skillet grease, but every night we have to shut them down to back-up the day's files."

"Well, can't you check out Taj before you do the back-up?" I asked.

"Sorry, son," the cop replied with a smirk. "But we just turned off our system five minutes ago." Behind him Fatso began laughing.

Because Taj is more organized and responsible, me and Yogi had given him all our money to hold onto. Now the cash was locked up with his wallet in a police vault. That meant we didn't have enough money to rent a hotel. When we got our car back me and Yogi drove it to the parking lot of Best Tires and tried to sleep in the back seat. It was around negative five degrees out so between our shivering and the cramped quarters me and Yogi found it impossible to doze off for more than about five restless minutes. Finally, near two a.m. the fatigue caught up with us and we fell into deep snooze. At two-thirty, a siren yanked us awake. As I wiped grimy sleep biscuits from my eyes I realized the car was bathed in a bright white light. Red lights were also flashing. I crawled from the car with my hands up. The thin cop walked through the spotlight chuckling.

"Sorry, boys," he said. "But this is private property. You can't sleep here. Besides, loitering is against the law in this town."

So we got back in the car and drove around Spread Eagle looking for someplace else to sleep. Finally, as I began to nod out at the wheel, I pulled into the parking lot of the local grocery store and killed the engine. I think we were asleep before I even finished pulling the parking brake.

Fifteen minutes later my nocturnal silence was again shattered by a siren. The thin cop's silhouette was grinning in the squad car spotlight. He repeated verbatim what he had said less than an hour before. I grudgingly started my car and moved on. The exhaustion felt like a new layer of skin, impeding my movements, weighing me down.

We parked behind a pizza place and the sleep tried to come back. But the sirens and lights did too. This time the cop didn't even need to say anything. I merely looked out the windshield and nodded at him as I started up the car. This scenario repeated itself about four or five times through the course of the night. For awhile the cop just followed us, making sure we didn't even try to pull over and sleep. Eventually, the sun came up, the cop's shift was over and he went home to his warm bed to sleep. Morning arrived and it was time to go pick up Taj.

Thankfully, they went ahead and let him out without torturing us with any more special checks. Taj seemed quiet and humble, I couldn't tell if he really felt this way or if it was the leftover of a facade he'd put up to help convince the cops to let him out sooner. Pigs, they know you hate their guts but they make you kiss their asses anyway.

"Hope you got a good night's sleep," I told him. "Your hotel accommodations were probably much more luxurious than ours."

"I didn't say anything to get in there and now that I'm out I'm not saying anything either," Taj replied coldly.

He stayed quiet for the next hundred miles, but me and Yogi couldn't keep our mouths shut. We kept ribbing him about bread and water and the buttfucking those cops must have given him. Yogi was in the back seat next to Taj, bombarding him with every chaingang cliche in the book, until Taj finally turned around and punched him in his chubby mug. After that Taj started talking again and we knew he was back to normal. It turned out Taj had had a hit of acid on him too, only when they put him in the white room he went ahead and ate it.

Our little exercise in modern fascism had cost us a lot of time. In order to make it to the wedding we had to drive straight on through to Montana without making any stops.

Luckily, the primer-mobile didn't suffer any breakdowns during that stretch. All the electrical tape I'd wound around her rusted parts seemed to be holding them together. The three of us, on the other hand, were falling apart. Cold and exhaustion had taken us hostage, reducing us to virtual zombies at the wheel. We drove in shifts, but our bodies were so sore and the car interior so cramped and musty it was impossible to sleep. The best you could hope for was an hour of deep trance. ACDC's *Back In Black* stayed in the tape deck for fifty-six consecutive playings, I figured that heavy metal sound would somehow act as an amphetamine. We kept smoking joints to clear our heads. During the home stretch we even ate a few hits of blotter just to keep ourselves awake.

Well, the wedding was one of those horrible religious affairs. The bride had to recite all these special vows where she promised to "submit herself totally to the will and guidance of her husband." I'm sitting there uncomfortable in my monkey suit thinking, Christ, Squiggy, why didn't you just hire a maid? Everyone in the church was completely uptight and Christian. I thought weddings were supposed to be happy, but these sour relatives were so serious I figured their faces would crack if it lasted a minute longer.

The reception was a blast. Me, Taj, and Yogi put on our leather jackets and got shit-faced. These people may have been religious but they could drink. The drunkest guy there was the dude the family had hired to videotape the whole affair. He was a sleazy Denver weasel all strung out on coke. High as Sputnik in a white tuxedo and talking blisters onto his tongue.

"Fuck these assholes," he said. "I've already been paid. Now I can party and fuck up as much as I want. Three thousand dollars for four hours' work. I'm not gonna have to get another job for a month."

He was so drunk he couldn't hold the camera steady. I

knew the tapes were going to come out all jiggly. He kept calling the bride's mother "Barge Butt" and the groom's father "Wrinkled Up Willy." The photographer pinched a great aunt on the tit and spilled one of his martinis over the head of a flower girl. After snorting two lines off the top of his video camera right in front of everyone he committed his ultimate faux pas. He was overflowing double vision and cocaine babble when the bride and father-in-law asked him to get a shot of them together. The photographer peered into the viewfinder and kept backing up trying to get them into focus but it was his eyes that were blurry, so he kept backing up and backing up till he backed right into the triple decker wedding cake, collapsing half of it. The little plastic bride and groom fell tumbling to the floor. And the weasel just stood there laughing, scooping handfuls of frosting off his ass.

We were almost afraid to drive back. The hundreds of miles and tall, ominous mountains reminded us of some dark gauntlet we had to run. Hiding in the folds of those peaks was a pig infestation, swarms of cops, scowling behind their radar like secret agents in mirrored shades. Besides that, a blizzard had begun and we had to follow a snow plow out of Missoula. The entire landscape was already soft, round, and blurred and the radio weatherman's reports sounded bleak as Nostradamus's prophecies of doom.

The snow plow dug a trough for ten miles out of town and we rode it the whole way. But when the plow U-turned back towards the city limits we were on our own and my bald tires crept into a dim polar terrain. The primer-mobile was the first to break the hymen ice on those blizzard roads. Nobody else was on the highway, nobody else was stupid enough to be driving under those conditions. Our reasoning was that we had to get back in time for winter session classes, although punctuality had never been a factor in our lives before and I had skipped forty-eight percent of my lectures during fall semester. I think we just wanted to get home. Away from the vulture fuzz and drooling hicks. Kerouac's idea of adventure lived on the highways but my fantasy book would have been titled *Off The Road.*

Three hours later we had managed to cover, oh, about thirty-three miles. Right before dusk, after getting stuck five times, we pulled into some little hillbilly convenience store and bought a cheap set of chains. The geeky old coot at the cash register just sat there over his space heater and laughed at us while we were putting them on. The chains were rusted and used. They lasted about a hundred miles before coming off in the drifts. Those cheap pieces of road velcro wouldn't show up again until the spring thaw.

By midnight the flakes were so thick I couldn't even see the end of my hood. There was no way to tell the road from everything else. We decided to pull off at a campground and wait out the storm. At least there wasn't a problem with finding any vacancies. The three of us ate some valium and passed out sitting up. A couple of times during the night I woke up in a fog bank of my own breath, feeling freezer burnt and shaking, and ran the heater until the car was warm enough to sustain human life again. In those cold patches of sleep I kept having a dream that a gaseous demon which I instinctively knew was pneumonia and flu virus kept chasing me around the inside of the car.

When we woke up the next morning the windows were completely covered with snow and ice. I had to take a wicked piss but when I tried to open the door it wouldn't budge. The damn thing was frozen shut. In a panic I roused Taj and Yogi and the three of us started kicking and pushing until the door handle bent and the window roller fell off, yet it still held like a bank vault. Our terror boiled up more adrenaline, booted feet frantic as jackhammers, until it finally made a metallic cracking sound and gave way outwards with a tumbling of snow and an inrushing of crisp fresh air. I ran out and wrote 'Sultan' in big yellow letters on the soft white. When I turned around and looked at the car it appeared to be buried under a bleached sand dune. If it weren't for the open door the vehicle would have been indistinguishable from any other hill. Snow had drifted at least three feet deep over the entire body. Where I was standing, it came up to my knees.

We spent the next hour digging the primer-mobile out with an old Prussian helmet Taj had left in the trunk. It only took us another two hours to get back to the main highway. The storm had pretty much passed, there were just a few leftover flurries to keep us paranoid. We made better time because large stretches of the road had been plowed. I had a couple of nasty skids but as far as I was concerned they just kept us on our toes.

By this point we didn't have quite so many drugs on us. We'd given Squiggy two ounces of sinsemilla, twenty hits of acid, and two quarters of mushrooms as wedding presents. Our stash was much smaller and at the rate we were consuming there was a fear that the bags might run dry before we hit California. The road is a harsh mistress and she demands strong medicine.

We were somewhere in the mountains driving past huge crags and jagged precipices. The primer-mobile was just flying, a big line of the Winnebago and RV crew behind us. Our elevation was somewhere near the tree line, snow on top of the peaks. There were a bunch of these warning signs along the road: CAUTION - FALLING ROCKS - BEWARE OF ICE, but we didn't see why they were there. It was a blue, crisp day. No snow or rain, the road was clear and dry. So we were cruising along about 75, passing all these license plates we noticed were local. Wonder why they're going so slow? Then the road cut through a narrow ravine between two huge ridges of rock and the asphalt turned to ice. The rear tires started going everywhere and we went into a spin, hit the guard rail, spun in the other direction. The Winnebagos were going crazy honking and swerving. We're all over the road spinning and sailing till I go straight off the shoulder toward this edge where I can't see anything beyond it. Does it just drop off sheer for two thousand feet? Are we gonna do the Hawaii 5-O cliff diving thing? My car goes flying airborne down this slope bouncing over rocks and bushes till about three acres down we come to rest against a boulder.

As the dust settles I'm just sitting there turning the key in my ignition going, "Well, at least my engine works." Front end's crumpled, headlights gone, and Taj keeps screaming, "Fuck! Fuck! Fuck!" Taj and Yogi climb out, Taj still going, "Fuck! Fuck! Fuck!" while I sit in the driver's seat and keep turning the key in the ignition, saying, "Well, at least my engine still works." And up the slope along the road a bunch of Winnebagos are pulled over and these gawking geeky country tourists get out in their down vests and sweaters, and start yelling down the hill with broad Northwest accents things like, "Hey, are you all alright?" And Taj just keeps jumping up and down screaming, "Fuck! Fuck! Fuck!"

The cops came by and wrote me out some tickets but didn't help us move the car. And, of course, the whole time I was talking to the officers Taj kept screaming, "Fuck! Fuck! Fuck!"

There was only one tow truck in the area and it belonged to Jim Bob and Bobby Jim. This was a tow truck that could survive World War III. The monster truck of tow trucks, the ultimate car mover. It was covered with a gaudy collage of Budweiser and STP oil stickers, redneck slogans like *I Love My Shotgun, Wee Doggie!* and *Ass Or Gas* had been painted on the pin-striped trim. The metal on the thing was so thick it could have stood up to armor-piercing shells.

They attached a big anchor type device to my poor demolished front end and started hoisting the car up the slope, bouncing it over rocks and evergreens like a waterskier hitting wakes. When we meet the brothers who own the truck we call them the "Chew Twins" cause they're both wearing these mechanics' uniforms with about fifty little pockets, and each pocket has got a bag of chewing tobacco or a round tin of Skol or Copenhagen in it. When we got in the truck with them they took off doing about ninety, drinking Jack Daniels and letting out these redneck Indian whoops, screaming, "Yee haw, Jimmy Bob, we gotta come back tonight and water the road agin!"

When we get to their filling station the brothers charge us three hundred dollars for the tow. One hundred to get my car up the hill, one hundred to drive it the two miles to the gas station (that's fifty dollars a mile!), and another hundred charged as a finder's fee. Finder's fee? We only had a hundred and twenty dollars between us. When I told the Chew Twins we couldn't afford it Bobby Jim said, "Well, how much money do you have?"

"One hundred and twenty dollars," I said dejectedly.

"Well, we'll just charge you for the finder's fee then," Jim Bob replied matter-of-factly.

And they took all the money we had. Between me, Taj, and Yogi there was about six bucks in change left to spend on gas to get back to San Francisco. Forget food. Here we were stuck with no money and a smashed car in Bum Fuck Nowhere with no place to stay in the middle of winter with snow everywhere, no food, no beer, no nothing. Plus, the front end had been bent so bad one of the wheels wouldn't turn. So we spent the rest of the afternoon in this slush-filled parking lot huffing and puffing with crowbars and pieces of metal trying to bend the front end enough that the tire would clear.

The whole time we're out there working in the cold the two assholes who run the station are sitting behind the glass doors and windows in the front room watching us from the warmth. And this town, probably got a population around sixty, is so boring that the Chew Twins invite over all their fat redneck buddies and they sit around in the office, pulled up to the heater, drinking beer and spitting chewing tobacco into cups, watching us bust our balls and freeze our asses. Occasionally one of them would open the door and yell out something like, "Heh, heh, yup, sure is warm in here."

Finally we managed to bend the bodywork so the car could drive. But the sun was going down and our headlights were gone. This left us no choice but to spend the night in Bum Fuck, frostbiting our asses sleeping in the back of the car. I woke up around four a.m. after a nightmare that our plane had crashlanded in the Andes and I had to eat Taj and Yogi's flesh to survive. It was so cold I couldn't feel my fingertips or toes. Only I couldn't start the car to run the heater because we needed every drop of gas for the ride back. There was an open Pepsi on the dashboard so I grabbed it and tipped it back but all the liquid in the can was frozen solid.

The next morning Taj remembered he had stashed an extra twenty bucks under the back seat, and went out and bought a couple headlights. Of course when we installed them it became apparent that something strange had happened to our electrical system because as soon as the engine turned over both bulbs exploded.

So we got on the road and just started driving. California, here we come!

That afternoon the three of us dropped some acid just to keep up our stamina. Although the blotters did keep us awake I think they may have impaired our decision-making process because when the sun went down we decided to keep driving. Who needs headlights? If we were careful, we reasoned, it would be possible to get in front of the big rig trucks and pace them, using their huge lamps and foglights as our own. I think subconsciously we couldn't face the prospect of sleeping in the car another ice cold night, better to press on, keep going till our gas ran out. But this idiotic plan forced one eighteen-wheeler after another into being our unwilling tailgater. When they tried to pass the pesky primer-mobile we'd speed up and change lanes with them to maintain our position. Sometimes it became a continual game of asphalt cat and mouse. The truckers would honk their horns, we'd just ignore them. Good thing we didn't have a CB because I'm sure the airwaves were filled with a corrosive commentary on us. The acid was shattering everything into tracers. Pink Floyd on the tape deck.

I remember this one mountain pass almost opaque with fog. We were going seventy miles an hour, floating about ten feet off the front bumper of an angry tank truck. The driver behind us had gotten so frustrated he began to shift gears so his metal monster made gestures of ramming. Those white headlights shined through the fog banks and pot smoke in the car in a way that reminded me of the laser light shows at a rock concert. I began air-guitaring to a Hendrix lead on the tape deck until the car swerved dangerously close to the guard rail. Taj and Yogi were in a trance, contemplating the inner and outer universes. With an unexpected burst of speed the trucker tried to pass us, but I overtook him and kept our car in the light. The whole thing made me feel like a remora.

Sometimes a truck would succeed in passing the primer-mobile, putting down the hammer till we couldn't catch up. With our eyes gone we'd pull over to the shoulder and spend a few minutes talking about the profound significance of dashboard knobs until a new victim came by. Then when a glow edged round the corner we'd swoop out and stick to it as we worked our way toward the dawn.

We spent New Year's Eve in Eugene, Oregon. By that point me, Taj, and Yogi didn't care anymore. It was time to go out and get fucked up. We were in a little better shape. At some logger bar in northern Oregon we had sold ninety dollars worth of pot. A family auto store outside of Portland had yielded a set of headlights which didn't spontaneously combust. True, the bulbs joggled around like a set of springy eyeball glasses, but at least they lit up the road. We had managed to skimp and save enough money so that the New Year could be a real blowout. The three of us started drinking our way in a white smear across town. Torqued up and raging.

At some country western bar a bunch of high school jocks tried to beat us up, but when we offered to get stoned with them their mood shifted three hundred and sixty degrees and an hour later we were all best friends and they were buying us tons of drinks. Taj, Yogi, and me left the bar around twelve and started driving back to the hotel we had rented for the night, blowing a big doobie on the way. Just when the primer-mobile had filled with smoke there ignited behind us the familiar lights of a squad car. By this time we've got it down to an art form. I open the vents, Taj and Yogi crack the windows and all that Eau De Humboldt goes blowing off into the cold night air. When the officer walks up, my window's down and I'm smiling my silly smile, and even wearing one of the dumb hick hats I bought in a local store. A pinch of chewing tobacco made my breath gross but legal.

"Do you realize your tags are expired?" the cop barked.

My tags expired at midnight on December 30th, 1991. It was now 12:15 on January 1, 1992. Fifteen minutes into the new year. I'm thinking, God, won't they ever cut me an inch of slack?

"But, officer," I whined. "They've only been expired for a few minutes. We're on our way back to California to get the car re-registered right now. We would have already been there if the car hadn't been in an accident."

"Drinking, I suppose," the officer sneered.

"Naaa, we just hit some ice."

"Are you calling me a liar?!" the cop screamed.

"No!"

"No, sir!"

"No, sir," I corrected myself. "Look, we just want to go

down there to our hotel so we can go to sleep."

"Which hotel?" he asked suspiciously.

"The Triple Star Motor Lodge. It's only about three blocks that way."

The officer still didn't look pleased. He took all our IDs and did another satellite check on us back in his car. I was beginning to think we'd be the first people to show up on post office Wanted posters without ever having committed a crime. Of course, he didn't find anything. Maybe a long record of how much we'd been harassed. Finally he gave back our licenses and said, "Okay, you're free to go. But you guys better go straight to your hotel. And remember, I'm watching you."

We started the car and pulled back onto the road. The cop fell in behind us and tailgated our trunk with his roof lights flashing. I don't know, maybe it was because I was paranoid from being pulled over, maybe it was because I was drunk, but I made a wrong turn, so instead of going only three blocks, we ended up driving about thirty miles for the next forty-five minutes, completely lost on all these dark roads. The pig was glued to our ass the whole time. I could just hear him back there, muttering to himself, "I know these boys are up to something."

Finally we pulled over and asked the cop for directions to the Triple Star Motor Lodge. "Look, I'm sorry," I told him. "I'm from out of town. I'm not trying to be a smart ass." He called in to his dispatcher and had them look the place up in the phone book. Even after telling us how to get there he followed our car all the way back.

When me, Taj, and Yogi got to the room we couldn't sleep and sat up with the lights off, in the glow of the TV set, blowing one hits into a wet towel and drinking beers. Occasionally we'd get up and peer through the closed blinds, wondering when the police state would close in on us again.

And all night long it was fucking freezing in that room. No matter how high we turned up the heat, the room temperature couldn't get above forty degrees. I remember when Yogi finally passed out his snores were blowing steady puffs of mist. The next morning when the three of us woke up shivering and coming down with colds I crawled into the bathroom and saw what the problem was. There was no glass in the bathroom window! The entire pane had been removed.

When we tried to hassle the pasty-faced guy who owned the place to get back some of our money he flew into a rage.

"Are you saying you thugs broke out my bathroom window?!?" he screamed. "You're lucky I don't call the police! Get out of here, you criminals!"

"Okay! Okay!" I apologized, holding my hands up to calm him down. "Just forget about it. We're leaving." Sheesh. Some places you just can't win.

When we got back to the city I wanted to fall down and kiss the greasy curb at Sixteenth and Mission. Thank God, or any of the many gods in San Francisco, to be in a place where the cops had real crimes to fight, and didn't go around making them up from their own paranoid fantasies. Back in the land of nose rings, smart drugs, and Cat In The Hat ravers. Where crack, pot, and acid were sold openly on the streets. Where bald-headed girls and transsexuals could get a job easily. Sure, it was dangerous here, but not as deadly as the peace officers in less exotic places. So give me the dirty cracked concrete, freaks, and lousy underground bands. The sticks give me the heebee-jeebies, so this skin is sticking to the streets.

The Rise and Fall of Third Leg

I will sing of Third Leg, the rise and fall, of one of the scummiest little punk rock bands to ever shit-smear the face of a college town. We had everything: drugs, sex, homosexuals. Why, our big hit was a tune called *Fudgepacker*. We inspired a riot, fist fights, philosophical debates, and expressions of food. Sorority girls threw beer mugs at us, and slept with the lead singer later. One night a drunken football jock threw a two hundred pound spool of electrical wire through the front door of one of our parties. I also remember the feedback rage. Jam sessions so hard I finished with only one string left on my guitar. Hell, I was the guitar player and I didn't even own a guitar for three months after I smashed my Sears no-name at the end of *No Cops* at a Skid Row gig. After that, at every show we played I jammed on a different axe. Everything was fluid in that band. To us, rock and roll meant doing drugs and getting laid, the two basics of youth, and we were ready to ride Third Leg as long as it would last. It was the early '80s, the new punk rock bands let us know you could do anything on a stage, and Third Leg was one of those rare groups of people who underneath all the bullshit and hype really just wanted to take off their clothes and roll around in the music, the instruments, and the speaker wires until they electrocuted themselves.

Everything started the spring of my sophomore year in college. I had been playing electric guitar in my dorm room on a cheesy little dime store amp. I took the avant-garde approach, learning to make weird noises with the strings, some days I just played with the species of feedback I could generate. I loved the high shrieking tones that sounded like birds. Around that time this polyester guy started showing up, saying we were going to be in a band. He wore loud leisure suits that looked like something a sleazy used car dealer would wear. He had both ears pierced (which was very radical at the time) and would often wear two earrings, one said FUCK and the other said YOU. His name was Jim Whiny but I'll always know him as Dada Trash. He said he played the drums.

Dada Trash turned out to be a much better drinking partner than a drummer. For the rest of that spring we hung out together and became good friends. Like most college sophomores we drank all the time, and Dada Trash had a great social network when it came to finding out where the parties were. Usually when we drank we talked about the band we were going to form. We spent hours discussing what our name, style, and ideology would be. Of course we never spent even five minutes actually practicing or trying to write songs. But I didn't mind. Dada Trash was great company. He was funny, insightful, and he had the weirdest wardrobe on campus. His closet was filled with gaudy leisure suits and he insisted that they would all be valuable collector's items when the '70s disco look came back into fashion. He would wear elevator shoes and fuzzy yak hair jackets to his classes. Nobody on campus even remotely resembled Dada Trash. He was a one man fashion statement. I remember when he went through his '60s-suburban-housewife stage. For an entire month he wore nothing but women's stretch polyester pantsuits and plastic glow-in-the-dark baubles. As an added touch he often wore eyeliner or lipstick. He would have come off as a transvestite were it not for his constant three day beard growth. The end result was equal parts kitsch and mutation. Contrary to what one might believe, Dada Trash was straight. But his wardrobe had a tendency to cause trouble. One incident in particular sticks in my brain.

It was a Friday night, and me and Dada Trash had been pounding beers at a party in the Towers apartment complex. Around twelve-thirty the keg ran dry so someone had to go on a brew run to keep the festivities rolling. Dada Trash had his parents' El Camino for the weekend so he offered to go. Five minutes later me and Dada were driving towards Sam's Bar and Grill at seventy miles an hour. But we were too late. Bars in Delaware close at one a.m. This meant we had to venture into the wilds of Maryland which serves alcohol until two. Out in the sticks we found some little white house bar loaded to the brim with rednecks and good ole boys who all musta been sloshing down about their second case. We went in and I walked up to the bartender, laid down a twenty spot, and told him to stack up as many cases as it would buy. While he was collecting them, all these grits were throwing spitballs at Dada Trash, calling him a queer because of his pink mohawk haircut and powder blue leisure suit. I was so drunk I was oblivious to it all. But when I was walking out with the cases some guy in a Cat Diesel hat screamed, "Git the fuck out of here, faggots!" and I turned around and yelled, "Motherfucker, I'm as heterosexual as they come!" Dada Trash dragged me out the door while the guy in the Cat Diesel hat sat there going, "Hetera-what?"

We got out to the El Camino and I had to take a leak so I started pissing on this car beside us. Then I looked up and saw that I was pissing right in front of this huge picture window in the side of the bar with all these rednecks in it pointing at my piece of manhood and shaking their fists at me like they're about to go lynching. Before I knew what was happening about half the bar came streaming out the front door, cussing and throwing bottles at us. Needless to say, I shoved it in quick, hopped in the car and we wheeled out of there like Bigfoot was chasing us. As beer bottles broke against the rear bumper I was hanging out the passenger side window screaming, "Eat shit, rednecks! Eat shit!"

When we got back to the party me and Dada Trash started talking again about the kind of band we were going to start but all those grandiose plans and even, it seems, the rest of that semester just kind of dissolved in the bottom of a can of Budweiser.

It wasn't until the next fall that we got a band together. Our name was Virgin Potato, and boy, did we suck. Our first gig was at a keg party and we set up right next to the keg, hoping this would assure us a captive audience. But we played so bad that not only did everyone leave the room, they dragged the keg out with them. The only person who stayed there to watch was our friend Chaos, who remained because he had eaten three quaaludes and was too blitzed to even stand up. He passed out during our second song. We only played about five gigs and at three of them Dada Trash didn't have any drums and kept the beat by banging on wooden tables and chairs with kitchen utensils.

I remember one afternoon when me and Pip were jamming in someone's living room, trying to come up with a few tunes. It was the two of us and another three or four people who were just sitting around getting stoned. We had been playing for a couple of hours and were getting to that sour end of the jam stage where both of us were out of tune and getting tired, fingers cramping, and the music just sounded like shit, when Dada Trash burst into the room screaming at the top of his lungs and shoved a microphone into his pants. This made him look like he had a huge erection and caused the microphone to feedback loud as banshee screams. He ran up to the amplifier and pretended to fuck it, causing an unholy racket. As we kept up the rhythm section Dada Trash proceeded to play a feedback lead with his crotch until everyone was laughing so hard the tune just fell apart.

Probably the most interesting thing about Virgin Potato was how we got our name. One day when I was in the dining hall this guy I knew put his hand in his pants and stuck the forefinger out through his fly so it looked like a dick. He then proceeded to 'fuck' a potato on his lunch tray. The potato was on a red napkin and when he poked his finger all the way through the potato some of the red dye came off. So when he pulled it out it looked like there was blood all over the end of his finger. "Look, it's a virgin!" someone screamed. "A virgin potato!" When Dada Trash heard this story he insisted we name the band that.

As entertainment went, well, we were good at clearing a room. That winter the death knell fell on Virgin Potato when Dada Trash moved out to LA to become famous. But like so many others in the big city, he just got lost in the crowd, got all spaced out and was last seen wandering around Venice Beach in a nehru jacket with a photo of Michael Jackson scotchtaped to his forehead.

Through the rest of that spring I continued to play music with the bass player, Pip. My training in music followed directions more akin to Darwin's Theory of Evolution than the melodic blasphemies of music theory. By summer I had come to the conclusion that the guitar is a percussion instrument. That spring passed pleasantly, as me and Pip made jangly sounds in his apartment. Sometimes Pip would play his bass by pounding on it with a stainless steel wrench. We were learning how to play our instruments and it was a time of infinite growth. We began to realize how volume can cover up a lack of talent. Sure, it bothered the neighbors but a key part of rock and roll, we reasoned, was the need to bother the neighbors.

Later on in the spring, me and Pip came up with this four chord progression that really just hit it. We played the riff over and over, for a half-hour at a time, the tune seemed to have a life of its own. I had such a feel for the progression that I worked out great leads, I could jam it out in feedback fluxes, straight notes, steel slide, or by banging the strings with a chicken drumstick. This was the first song me and Pip had ever done that we really knew was good. It let us know that maybe there was a future to this whole thing. Little did we realize those four chords would evolve into *Fudgepacker*, Third Leg's biggest hit.

That summer everyone went back home to their parents' houses and worked lousy part-time jobs. I spent the hot months washing dishes, smoking bad homegrown, and hammering out riffs. My parents owned a modern house which had a living room almost two stories high. The outside wall of the room was all glass and looked out on some lush green woods. Whenever my parents left the house I would set up my guitar and amp in the middle of the living room, turn the volume up all the way, and jam for the trees. There was a certain transcendence I reached during those summer jams. During certain rhythms and riffs I would fall off into a trance-like state and start drooling on the fret board. There was a high clear ringing sound I could get in that room, it was a volume thing. Sometimes I played so loud that I could swear the leaves outside the window began to shake.

The next fall when we went back to school me and Pip met up with Brian Box. Brian was a real musician. He was a music major specializing in classical arrangements. He played six or seven different instruments. Brian not only read music but was taking courses in advanced composition. Me and Pip couldn't figure out why he wanted to work with us. We had only been playing our instruments for about a year. Neither of us could read music. I couldn't even play bar chords for chrissakes! But Brian was really into starting a band with us. He was downright enthusiastic about it. Even though its history had been a short one, Virgin Potato was a band whose name continued to live in local infamy. I could sense that Brian was getting tired of his stuffy symphonies. Like musicians of any age he wanted to get into the 'now' sound, and he sensed it was lurking somewhere in our primitive riffs. We were skeptical about all this, but in the end me and Pip were just glad we had a real musician who was willing to play with us.

Our first practice took place in the basement of the International House, which was a dormitory for foreign students. That night we achieved a decibel level somewhere around eighty or ninety and I don't think there was a distinguishable melody in the entire four hour practice. The next week when the three of us showed up to practice again we were met by a multinational force which looked like it had been sent by the United Nations. We were told in a medley of languages that our presence would no longer be tolerated in the International House. We protested, of course, but most of our accusers could not speak English and therefore could not comprehend our justifications, philosophical excuses, and political pleas for freedom of speech and sound. Far from being discouraged by this, the three of us felt a new determination as we left the International House that night, for we realized our music spoke louder than words and transcended all ethnic and national boundaries.

The next week we practiced in the student lounge of my dorm. And got kicked out of there with explicit instructions to never return. The week after that we practiced in the student lounge of Pip's dorm. This time the campus police showed up and warned us that if they ever heard us playing there again we would be slapped with a noise violation, evicted from the dorms, and have to pay a stiff fine. We couldn't understand it. We had turned our volume level down to only sixty or seventy decibels. All the legends were true. The authorities really did hate rock and roll. They would systematically try to stomp it out anywhere it showed up. What was everybody's problem? We were just trying to jam.

Finally our band found a stable practice space at Brian's

place. Brian lived in the Music House, a large dormitory building which only housed music majors. The house had no immediate neighbors and inside its walls students could practice their instruments without fear of harassment from the authorities. I remember the first night me and Pip entered the place, lugging our amps and guitars. Brian lived on the top floor and as we trudged up the stairs we passed open rooms where string quartets played Mozart. A black kid in a beret plucked out Monk standards on a stand-up bass. A pimply faced girl with red pigtails played sweet baroque music with a flute. On the third floor a fat boy wearing a Kansas t-shirt puffed on an immense tuba. Then me and Pip walked into Brian's room, plugged in our amplifiers, and made fifteen minutes worth of pure noteless feedback. By the end of this, every denizen of the Music House was lined up outside Brian's door screaming, "That's not music!" Brian met them with a calm but determined poker face. "Yes, it is," he said, and to prove it he began playing french horn along with me and Pip's formless shrieks.

Back then I thought music was just sound. There was a subtle beauty in all the shapes of noise. I thought being a good guitarist meant playing a lot of notes, and it didn't matter if they were plucked in any specific order. I began to look at rhythm as merely an abstract form of abuse. Keys were for opening doors. And melody was a dirty word. If one began to embrace melody it was just a matter of time before they became that Greatest Of All Satans: Top Forty.

Brian Box seemed to love it all and that was validation enough for me. I had faith in his knowledge and expertise. He was one of those people who could pick up any instrument and music just seemed to bleed out of it. In one of our songs me and Pip would play rhythm by banging on our bass and guitar strings with Pepsi cans while Brian played floral violin themes from Beethoven over top. Later on, when Third Leg was performing live, we played that tune by pounding on the strings with beer cans and the song would be over when one of the cans exploded. But for the most part Brian played the drums. He played them because percussion was an instrument he had yet to completely master and because it was the most sorely needed position in the band. He loved polyrhythms and revelled in creating rich backgrounds of beat. Pip owned a programmable drum machine which Brian loved to employ. Usually he programmed in a complex rhythm that could have stood well enough on its own, but Brian used it as just the seed or core, and surrounded it with lush branches of rolls and beats as he played along on a full drum set. Brian played drums so well his rhythms were melodies.

Over top of his intricate structures me and Pip laid down an industrial wasteland of noise, feedback, and dissonance. Most of our lyrics were a general screaming about the disintegration of the modern world and the alienation of youth. From a political and cultural standpoint it was challenging stuff, but if analyzed from the perspective of music theory, well, it was total gratuitous garbage.

As one might expect, our Dadaist experiments in sound began to wear thin on the residents of the Music House. Graffiti began to appear in the bathrooms deriding us as 'unlistenable crap', 'total shit', 'just plain noise', and a host of other unflattering terms that plainly revealed the jealousy of musicians who didn't have an original sound. One of my favorite descriptions pegged us as 'aural masturbation'. Obviously just the childish rantings of inferior minds. All of them lacked our vision.

But it went beyond that. The first and second floors organized a committee to have us evicted from the house. Every day Brian came home to find his door covered with nasty notes. Finally a house meeting was called to discuss the matter. As soon as me, Pip, and Brian walked into the gathering it was obvious the situation amounted to the entire house against the three of us. Everyone instantly began yelling that they had had it up to here. Playing the devil's advocate, I asked them where 'here' was, did it have a specific decibel level?

"Here," replied the tubby tuba player from the third floor, "is where the music is turned up so loud that feedback occludes it to the point where one can no longer distinguish notes or melody."

"But isn't that where the future of music begins?" I said.

"What you all play isn't music, it's just noise," snapped the pimply faced girl with the red pigtails.

"Hey, when Stravinsky first played his compositions people called it noise," replied Pip. "But history has proven them wrong."

"There's no conceivable way you guys can compare yourselves with Stravinsky," snapped a blond boy wearing a *Rock Me Amadeus* t-shirt.

"Hey," Brian Box said. "I thought this whole house was set up to be conducive to freedom of expression. How can you all censor us without negating everything this place stands for?"

There was a moment of silence as everyone pondered this point.

Not wanting to lose the advantage, me and Pip launched into a prepared speech defending our right to rock based on certain inalienable rights laid down in the Constitution and the First Amendment. If America was truly a free country then we should be allowed to let our decibels fly like flags on the breeze. We went on for about five minutes and when it was all over the black guy in the beret calmly said, "You two have no rights in this situation since you're not residents of the Music House."

But Brian was a resident. He came to our defense in one of the most stirring speeches I have ever heard. It was a proclamation of artistic freedom. He quoted Abraham Lincoln, Malcolm X, Beethoven, and Elton John. For a full fifteen minutes he delivered an eloquent manifesto on the need for uncensored expression and how all attempts to restrain and control music have inevitably led to fascism.

"The span of music is as limitless as the human imagination," he said at one point. "Every culture that has embraced music has radically transformed its structures and phrasings into shapes that are sometimes completely unreadable to other civilizations. But they are no less valid. To say that they are invalid would invalidate all music. There is no one standard. To put a limit on music would be to put a limit on the human imagination. And we all know you cannot do that. It's why we became music majors. To find the promise, to ever delve into the new, to create. The art form has evolved for millennia. It will go on till eternity. What one man, school, or even society, can claim to set its boundaries? You know in your hearts that there is no limit to the beauties of music, which is why a vote against my band here today is really a vote against yourselves and your ability to grow as individuals."

When Brian was done no one said anything. There was nothing they could say. Because he was right, damn it! In the end we got to keep practicing at the Music House, but by way of compromise we had to turn the volume way down. At first this bothered us a lot, but hey, a place to jam is a place to jam.

Our first gig occurred at a keg party in Ivy apartments. A series of thesaurus-style meetings between me, Pip, and Brian had proved fruitless so we ended up performing as The Band That Cannot Be Named. Since me and Pip were always stoned or drunk while we practiced, we figured it would be best to be inebriated while on stage, too. Brian, on the other hand, was a 'straight edge', which meant he did not drink or do drugs. We couldn't even get him to drink Pepsi since it contained caffeine which Brian called "one of the most dangerously underrated drugs of the twentieth century." In many ways, Brian resembled an adult boy scout.

At this point there were only three people in the band

and we set up in one corner of the living room. Me and Pip were not about to have everyone walk out on us this time. We turned or amplifiers up so loud everyone in the apartment complex could hear us and we tied the keg to Brian's drum set. Only this time the audience didn't vacate the premises. I don't think they knew what to make of us, but they stood there and watched the entire set. I had had diarrhea all day from a case of stage jitters. Pip wasn't in much better condition. Brian though, who was an old pro at performing live, was ultra-psyched and couldn't wait to go on. He was smiling this big white grin and kept saying, "I can't believe I'm finally going to get to play the drums on stage!"

After me and Pip had downed about five beers each and the hour hit midnight, we decided it was time to go on. Pip and I strapped on our instruments of destruction and Brian picked up his sticks. There was a short moment of silence as we stared out at the audience. We took a deep breath and launched into one of the most explosive sonic tidal waves anyone there had ever heard. I just remember the huge white noise of it all, Brian's drums pounding into my back like punches from a boxer. My hands flew up and down the strings playing as fast as I could, not caring about the timing or melody. I figured if I just played fast enough no one would worry, the pure speed would snap back their heads. Pip was also surging forward like a wild bull, strangling his bass as if it were a snake trying to escape him. After about three minutes the tune settled into a steady humming velocity. I rose up out of my fog. So did Pip. I looked over at him. "What song are we playing?" I yelled through all the noise. "I don't know," said Pip, shaking his head and shoulders in a way that let me know he was completely lost. Things went downhill from there.

I don't think me and Pip played the same song at the same time once during that entire first gig. Each progressive tune was more of a crackling chaos than the one before it. We hadn't written out a set list so everything was haphazard.

About halfway through the set Pip and I tried to decide what the next tune would be during the few patches of silence. Unfortunately, Brian's ears were ringing so loud he couldn't hear what we were saying and he would start into the tune before we had reached a consensus. Even when me and Pip figured out what we were playing between the two of us, inevitably we were too drunk and stoned to remember exactly how the song went. The end result was a cacophonous waste of epic proportions that at times was nothing more than a guttural hum of feedback. "If you play fast enough it will be good," I kept telling myself, and after awhile I gave up the structure of the songs entirely and just tried to put as many notes into the three to five minute patches of noise as I could possibly bang out on my guitar. At best, I hoped people in the audience would mistake the tangled mess for jazz improvisation. Their expressions ranged from puzzlement to horror. At one point I looked up during an especially loud shriek of feedback and everyone in the room had their fingers in their ears.

Brian was singing almost all the tunes, but his mike was so low in the mix you could hardly hear his vocals. Only a few words made it through the jungle of chewing noises. "Kill... Baby you're... Fudge... Ronald Reagan's colon..." appeared here and there, strange flowers on a field of explosions. Toward the end some guy walked out of the audience and began to sing into Pip's mike. He stayed there and sang the next four tunes. The audience seemed to actually like what he was saying though I couldn't hear a word of it.

Finally the songs broke down into infernal stuttering sparks. We ended with one final frantic blast of white heat that lasted about five minutes and was all over the place. Then it was finished. The audience seemed stunned by the sudden silence. The whole set had only lasted a half-hour. Outside the living room windows I could see the flashing lights of police cars pulling up to the apartments. It had been the longest half-hour of my life.

The three of us walked into the crowd in a daze. Our bodies had been physically battered by the high decibels, our ears were ringing so loud we could hardly hear what anyone said. The verdicts appeared to be mixed.

"Total garbage," said someone.

"Awesome, man! Totally hardcore," said someone else.

"Was there a hook in that? Or a riff? Or a note?"

"That was the most industrial thing I've ever seen."

"Like Hendrix, only on meaner drugs," someone said as they patted me on the back.

"That was the worst show I've ever seen. You couldn't even call it music. It was an atrocity."

"Well, you're no Michael Jackson, but it was okay." I didn't know what to make of the whole thing. All the comments seemed to be conflicting. This was back when I still took criticism seriously.

It turned out that the guy who had come up and started singing with us while we were playing was Jimmy Shred, a local skateboard pro and all around man about town. Brian went up to him after the show and was radioactively ecstatic. "Man," Brian said. "I don't know what you were saying to those people, but they seemed to be eating it up! That was just totally extemporaneous! Radical!"

We didn't find out until later that what Jimmy was singing about was how much he wanted to pick up this blonde girl in the back and the audience was amused by it because he was making a complete ass of himself.

"What a way to work a crowd," Brian raged. "You've got great stage presence. How'd you like to be our lead singer full time?"

"Sure," Jimmy Shred said. "Where do I sign?"

Brian pulled up his shirt and handed Jimmy a ballpoint pen. Jimmy signed his name across Brian's stomach. Then they shook on it. From then on, Jimmy was our front man, right up to the bitter end.

Back then me and almost everyone I knew smoked pot

constantly. Getting stoned was as common as saying hello. Alcohol wasn't even considered a drug yet. It was just a different form of water. At the end of my freshman year I calculated that I had tripped fifty-five times over the course of the year, at least once a week, and some of these experiences involved consuming five or more blotters.

This was the early '80s. There was a hedonistic spillover from the '70s which kept people drunk with their legs spread open. The severity of AIDS hadn't sunk in yet, coke was just catching on, fueling the people up, getting them ready for the big tidal wave of greed that was about to hit. Third Leg had problems in this department. Our lead singer, Jimmy Shred, had a little nose habit sponsored by a local coke dealer, Big Bobby Brody. We just called him BBB. Sometimes this stood for Blow, Booze, and Babes. He was kind of a sponsor of Third Leg for awhile. He gave us a little extra incentive for our live shows. Unfortunately, because of his naturally sociopathic personality, Jimmy Shred always eeled an extra three or four lines out of BBB, and on stage Jimmy would be going about 78 rpm while the drummer and the rest of us were hanging at 45 rpm, and usually he'd finish the tunes about two measures ahead of everyone else. Strangely enough, some people thought this made his vocals 'real punk rock' and it added to his allure as a front man.

But the best thing Jimmy Shred had going for him was that he was a cute young blonde punk rock boy who was a skateboarding pro. He had a cute ass and all the local new wave girls would scream out for him at our shows in fits of hormonal psychosis. Jimmy got laid more than the rest of us even though he had a full-time girlfriend for the first half of the history of the band. After awhile though, his flesh flow washed her off like an old barnacle.

And if Jimmy Shred was our lead singer you knew New Wave Dave couldn't be far behind. New Wave Dave was Jimmy Shred's best friend, hell, he was his sidekick. Like Batman and Robin, the Lone Ranger and Tonto, Bogey and

Bacall. Of course Dave was also blonde. Jimmy Shred considered brunettes a lower life form. As a result, all of his inner circle were either naturals or they had a good peroxide job. I'm a red head so they didn't know what to make of me. But anyway, New Wave Dave had to join the band, whether there was a place for him or not. I didn't mind, 'cause Dave was actually much cooler than Jimmy. He had great taste in music, beer, and women. He was tall, over six feet, and good looking in a big galoot kind of way. Even though he couldn't read music, had never picked up an instrument, and couldn't sing, he brought enormous enthusiasm to Third Leg.

At first we had him singing backup vocals. This worked out okay, but after awhile Dave complained that he didn't have enough to do on stage. So we let him play bass. Yes, Third Leg had two bass players. While Pip played the real rhythm, Dave would pluck out hyper-simplified one note versions of the songs. Unfortunately, Dave's ears were solid tin and sometimes he'd stray so far off beat that other people in the band would start to follow him and whole songs would come to a crashing dissonant halt. Now these errors weren't too apparent on stage because Third Leg was notorious for playing in two keys at once, but after awhile, those of us in the band who were slightly more musically inclined felt that something had to be done. By this time we were all good friends with Dave so it never crossed our minds to kick him out of the band. Instead we decided it would be best if Dave played on stage as usual but we wouldn't plug in his amplifier.

One time after a show a reporter asked me backstage, "I noticed tonight that your second bass player was running about, playing his heart out, but there wasn't a cord connecting his instrument to his amp, and I couldn't hear him in the mix."

"Well," I said. "For certain shows we feel it's best if Dave plays in a mime bass style. That was what first impressed us about him. He's an expert on silent music. And you know, for a bass player, he also plays a pretty good air guitar."

At some shows Dave just pretended to play a flat piece of cardboard that had a bass painted on the front of it. Toward the end Dave stopped even singing backup vocals and never actually made any sound during a show. But we didn't mind. Most of us were concentrating so hard on the notes we were playing that we didn't move around much on stage. Dave, on the other hand, wasn't so limited by the demands of structured sound. He could prance around, play his bass between his legs, behind his back; in short, do all the wild and crazy rock and roll moves that the rest of us couldn't attempt. There were shows where I saw him throw his bass spinning up into the air and then he'd catch it without there being a single interruption in the music. Even though Dave never made any sound we still kept him around because he just had such great stage presence.

I remember the first time me, Jimmy Shred, Pip, and New Wave Dave went to see a hardcore punk show. We'd been to rock concerts before and had seen a lot of garage bands who could have worn the punk label, but this was the first time we had ever been to a show that put itself forth as part of 'the scene'. People didn't throw the word 'scene' around as much back then as they do now. You have to remember the '70s had just ended. The stink of disco still hung in the air and all the radio stations played was lame oldsters like The Who, Beatles, and Rolling Stones. Don't get me wrong, those are good bands but enough was enough already. After hearing *I Wanna Hold Your Hand* every day for twenty years, how many more times can you listen to it? The big record companies had a virtual stranglehold on the whole music industry, and because new bands were a gamble that might lose them money they just kept regurgitating the same old shit. There was no such thing as 'alternative' music back then. That was, until punk rock came to America. Like many great music movements, the new sound started in England, in this case with the Sex Pistols. Everyone in America hated *Never Mind The Bullocks*. At least at first. I remember buying my copy of the album for ninety-nine cents from a cutout bin. It had only been released six weeks before. In those days, the cheapest cutout records you could find cost at least $3.95. So this piece of vinyl had to be a real dog. But I loved it. Not only that, many of my friends did too. We used to dance to it at parties in high school. There were other new bands around then, like Devo and the Talking Heads, but they could only penetrate so far into the American Mind. They were quirky, but they still relied too much on regular song structures and proper musicianship.

And then came punk rock. Though the whole thing can rightfully be traced back to the Sex Pistols, they were just the first ripple. What hit America a few years later was a tidal wave. Punk made music raw again, it brought us back to our roots. The songs were simple, loud, and sloppy. Anyone could play punk rock. And that was the whole point. You didn't have to be an accomplished and studied musician with a million dollar record deal if you wanted to play in a band, perform shows, and put out albums. Once again music was for Everyman. For the members of Third Leg, these concepts were a revelation. Because let's face it, we sucked. But in the new scene, that was okay. The important thing was to just keep doing it.

That first hardcore show opened up a whole new world for us. It showed us there were other people making music like us, and even better, there was an audience for this kind of sound. Sure, the whole punk thing didn't reach us hicks in Delaware till a couple years after it hit every place else but who cares? It still made just as big an impression on us. The point is, we eventually got it. Better late than never.

The show was on a Friday night up in Philly. Twitching Membrane, Sadistic Surgery, and Fetal Mistakes were playing in a gymnasium on the second floor of an old condemned school whose windows flickered green and blue over the blasted buildings and junkie alleys in the grittiest blocks around 30th Street. The whole area had a reddish glow over it from the city lights. Inside, the crowd was all spikers and mohawks wrapped in leather and chains. Some girl by the front door was wearing a black rubber slip and fishnet body suit. Her hair was a bright red and white candle flame flaring over thick cat-eye makeup, on her tit was a tattoo of a spiderweb with a cross woven into the strands. On the stairs, a pimply kid passed out in a sitting position had pissed in his pants and the stream of urine ran down three stairs to the next landing. To us, this was horrendous, marvelous squalor.

The dance floor was tropical hot, sweaty, soured with smoke, and beginning to growl as Sadistic Surgery sliced into their second set. Everyone in the band was wearing a t-shirt that said: *Kill 'Em All, Let God Sort Them Out*, and the music crackled and ran like an amphetamine scream. The songs were loud and twisted, snakes of feedback slithered through them. Words to describe the sound? Primitive. Rage. Frustration. Violence. There seemed to be some kind of explosion going on in the bodies in the crowd. The Nazi punks slamming like a drunken tribe. Swastikas and FUCK YOUs drawn on blackboards along the walls. A fifteen-year-old skinhead with an X cut into his scalp was talking about pissing in a girl's mouth. The machine gun of the drum. The serrated knife of a guitar feeding back. This was a primal sound that could have only come from caves, the caves of a city.

At one point, the lead singer of Fetal Mistakes caught a beer bottle in the face so he jumped off stage and beat the shit out of the spectator who threw it. Even once the guy surrendered, the lead singer kept picking him up and punching him back down to the floor again. The crowd parted to let them through. Like a vicious metronome, the singer ended up punching him all the way to the rear of the gymnasium. Behind them, a channel through the audience led back to the stage.

The music went on and on. A loud hornets' nest of sound. Slam dancers crushing studded leather against sweat and flesh, jumping up and crawling over backs and heads, rolling onto stage and then leaping out into space, their falls broken by clusters of grinding limbs. The whole room was a solid writhing mass. Sometimes the bodies would pile up in pyramids that rose high into the air before tumbling over and falling apart into a scramble. Tough bald girls were in it with the guys. Bruised slammers often had to crawl underneath the stage to get away from it all. The floor was a constant physical struggle.

I ran through the crowd screaming and colliding. My nose was bleeding and I loved it. The bass player was kicking faces along the front of the crowd when I rolled over a bunch of heads onto the flat surface beside him, turned, and dove from stage onto the snarling mass, crawling on all fours, bounced onto my back, bantered about the haircuts, then on my stomach, clawing to stay on top, swimming a sea of red spikes and pierced noses, then they rose up ten feet in a pile of muscles and I was riding the rage like the crest of a lawless wave, shaking my fist in the air.

Ah, I remember those days in the '80s. I was young, in college, away from my parent's home, out from under their thumbs, free, sexual, and just beginning to find out how big life is. I had a room to myself in a co-ed dorm, no supervision, the anti-drug hysteria of the Reagan years had not taken hold yet so the campus was literally flowing with a menagerie of stimulants. Up on Wall Street they were busy making millions but in the halls of academia we didn't care. We were too busy arguing philosophy, spending hours debating whether punk rock was a flashback of Dada or something totally new. Because I was young, my life seemed pure. I was experiencing things for the first time. The cynicism that would later take me over was only a seed back then. During the weeks I studied hard, but when Thursday night rolled around the open season began. Unless there was a test, Friday classes were a moot point. My attendance depended more on how much I had to drink on Thursday night than on the topic of the lecture.

I tried to keep my weekends a huge delirious chaos, and I fed off the anarchy. There was a tremendous rage inside me that bled out through the beer, parties, and women. Third Leg usually practiced on the weekends and the jam sessions were like a breakthrough. In the harsh simplicity of the chords and distortion I found a new and pure release. And even though what we made was ugly, it was still a form of creation. Through the medium of the guitar I let the violence inside me come out and then shaped it into songs. So many people around me seemed to be blinding themselves with drugs and alcohol but the music seemed to let us see things. I always thought it was truth I saw but it may have only been our ability to rise to our own potential.

The college I went to, University of Delaware, was a big school, over twenty-five thousand students. It was located in the town of Newark, and the student population almost equaled that of the town. The campus was effectively a city within a city. From my point of view, most of the student body was a vacuous bunch of suburbanites who had only come there to work on their alcoholism and pick up a pseudo-degree in their spare time. For the most part these people could be lumped into two categories: preppies and frat boys. Sororities wielded a lot of power among the female population, although many girls chose to be little sisters in fraternities. There was a small minority of brainy geeks who had come to the school to actually get an academic degree in the sciences, but these people seldom appeared outside of the library and their respective departments.

When I arrived at U of D, I got the impression that the

tyranny of the frats and preppies had reigned unchallenged throughout the '70s. But in the early-to-mid '80s a new group of people began to show up in Newark and at the University of Delaware. In hindsight I would call them punks, although at the time they didn't really know what to call themselves. They just knew they were different from the status quo. They were people searching for something and quite often they didn't even know what it was. This was the group I fell in among. It was the one social strata on campus where all the artists, writers, and musicians ended up. It was where all the thinkers held their conversations. Everyone in Third Leg was a 'punk', and we were conscious of the fact that we were shaping a different way of living. We knew we were outsiders and this gave us a sense of unity. It also gave us a good chance to form strong alliances with the other minorities on campus like the blacks and gays. When Third Leg played for their own crowd at a party, it was usually in a rundown living room that stank of stale keg beer and we looked out over a crowd of big hair gothic chicks, mohawks, afros, and screeching queens. Our groupies had names like Arnold Skinhead, Sue Real, and Screamer Joe.

By about 1984 the punks had taken over an entire street just off campus. The street was lined with cheap flea bag apartments owned and run by a notorious slumlord named Doctor Scarleg. Most of the punk bands in Newark resided and practiced in the living rooms of these hovels. People called the place Skid Row. Every Friday and Saturday night there would be a wild party in at least one of the row houses. Bands like Third Leg, Catherine the Great, and 1-800-Get-Down got their start at these beer bashes. By early '85 the scene had really gotten rolling and Skid Row was becoming a sort of cultural phenomena. Three or four houses along the street would give parties in tandem, with art installations in living rooms, and bands set up on a stage in the backyard.

That spring all the row houses got together and had the backyard of Skid Row carpeted. There were no fences separating the yards so it was one uninterrupted patch of ground. A city block's worth of cheap shag rug was bought and laid down behind the houses. This gave new meaning to the term 'indoor/outdoor'. The night they finished laying the carpet everybody threw a block party called The Great TV Smash Party. Five bands played. They held a raffle and the winner got to throw two TV sets off the roof. The drunken crowd cheered as the televisions fell spinning through the air and the picture tubes imploded. Glass went everywhere. Shards of it got stuck in the beehives of big hair girls who had used so much hair spray their dos were sticky as cotton candy. They didn't even pull the shards out, just left them there as a fashion statement.

There was a whole series of TV smash parties. Cute new wave girls who had won the raffle would put on safety glasses, walk up onto a stage in the backyard, and smash up ancient Magnavoxes with sledgehammers. Sometimes ten televisions were demolished at once in an orgy of sledgehammers, chain saws, shotguns, and exploding cathode ray tubes. People always cheered the destruction and violence. In the living rooms bands played till four or five in the morning, often mixing and matching with members of other groups to form jam sessions that wrung every bit of sweat from the musicians. Anyone was free to join in so the sessions often swelled to twenty or more people, with members of the audience sometimes stepping up to bang on drums or sing chorus. I remember looking up one Friday night at three a.m. to see that while I was playing lead guitar a group of Rastas had come in and were now frantically pounding away on congas and bongos. There was a delicious fluidity to the crowds which seemed to mimic the chaos of the alcohol flowing through us. It was a kind of freedom. We all thought that the anarchy we lived in our daily lives would one day grow so big it would escape us and infect the body of that great sleeping America.

Just after the two TV sets were thrown off the roof at the first TV Smash Party I remember seeing Zelda wearing her sad frown like a proud banner of neurosis. That night she was the attempted prey of Chaos, who had come dressed to impress with a hypodermic needle for a stick pin and a bicycle chain necklace stained by the bloody nose he had received while slam dancing. He tried to woo her with his stories of gang fights on Staten Island, but I knew it was a hopeless affair. Zelda never had sex with anyone she met while under the influence.

When someone said, "Hi, Zelda, how are you today?" she would usually reply in a lifeless monotone, "Miserable and in a state of moral decay, how about yourself?" She could twist a knife in any man's balls. One night, in Laweenie's Steak House and Pub, a horny Italian guy talking trash was animatedly trying to pick her up. For over twenty minutes he went on and on bragging about his prowess at drinking and fighting while Zelda sat there in complete silence. Finally, she looked over at him and said, "You are boring, leave me alone."

"What do you mean, I'm boring?" the guy said in complete shock. "I'm not boring at all. How can you say I'm boring?"

With a gaze of steel, Zelda stared him down and said, "The only thing more boring than a dull person is someone who talks about being boring."

Zelda dressed like the B-52s. She had a neon bright wardrobe of 1960s suburban wear polyester pants and tops, all of them bought at Goodwill. She loved to dress in eye-hurting color combinations like black and yellow striped shirts atop florescent fuchsia pants. And like the clashes of her outfits, her personality never lacked abrasiveness.

One night Zelda and her friends were kicked out of a party because she walked up to the host and for no reason said, "You're an asshole, and your party sucks." Five minutes later, on their way to another party, Zelda's friends tried to impress upon her the values of moderate behavior.

I remember when my friend, James Shut, a Jerseyite with hyper hormones, first met her at another Skid Row party. Later that night he spoke with me at the keg. "For twenty minutes she cut me down on all physical, mental, social, moral, and ethnic levels," he said. "I've never been so demeaned by another human being in my life. I'm in love."

As Zelda was leaving at two a.m. James asked if he could see her again.

"Maybe when I'm thirty-five I'll live with you for a couple of months," she said. "But until then, stay out of my sight."

James couldn't seem to purge her from his system and through the rest of that spring he sent her long syrupy love letters. Her response to these honest bearings of the heart was to spit on James whenever they ran into each other in public. After six months of this kind of treatment, James finally got the message and backed off.

For a while there both Chaos and Pip were obsessed with Zelda. This situation was further complicated by the fact that Chaos and Pip were roommates at the time. Neither seemed like prime candidates for Zelda's affection. Let me explain.

When Chaos was in college, he lived an incredibly Spartan existence. He had almost no possessions. Steering away from worldly goods was one of his primary focuses in life. Of course, Pip was a total slob. His side of the room was a trash heap full of dog-eared magazines, pin-up posters, unwashed laundry and moldy socks. But Chaos's half of the room was spotless and white. Nothing on the carpet, bare walls, no furniture. He kept his three outfits of clothing neatly folded along with a shoebox full of personal effects in a duffel bag next to his bed. The bed itself was just a bare mattress which he slept on in the nude. No sheets. Occasionally in the wintertime he covered himself with an army blanket. The only artwork Chaos owned, the only decoration of any kind that adorned his side of the room and expressed his personality hung on the wall just above the bed. It was a picture of Jesus Christ on a tiny piece of cloth was stuck to the wall by a hypodermic needle shoved through Christ's forehead and whenever Chaos jerked off he used it as a cum rag.

Often their competition for Zelda's attention reached such a fever pitch that they ended up having horrible fights. One time they had a fight lasting over four hours. The punches started in their living room and by the time the battle was over the two of them were a mile and a half away, slugging it out on the railroad tracks. Pip finally ended everything by pushing Chaos down. He sat on a railroad spike that punctured his butt and took ten stitches to close up. Zelda was rather touched by the whole situation and would often ask Chaos how his 'second asshole' was doing.

Pip actually went out with Zelda for a couple of months, though they never had sex. Zelda constantly paraded around Pip in suggestive lingerie or completely nude but whenever he tried to instigate conjugal situations she said the idea of having sex made her nauseous. Pip claimed to enjoy the relationship. There was an excitement to it that went beyond the merely physical. "Besides," he said. "As far as I'm concerned, humiliation is the only pure emotion."

After she broke up with Pip, Zelda met the one true love of her life, a man she would eventually marry. He was a political revolutionary named Jose. He had actually fought with the Sandinistas in Nicaragua, and was a never-ending fountain of polemic slogans. Zelda told Pip and Chaos that sex with Jose was fantastic, "like some kind of metaphysical rebirthing." She told them this at another Skid Row party and as the two of them listened to her I watched their faces shatter and collapse.

"I'm really sorry we acted like such idiots around you these past few months," Chaos said to her. "I guess me and Pip act so weird because we had fucked-up childhoods."

"Don't worry about it," said Zelda. "Everyone's childhood

warps them."

At that point both Pip and Chaos began crying, and turned around and hugged each other.

After Jimmy Shred and New Wave Dave joined the band we began to work on the music in earnest. Me and Pip were writing four or five songs a week. We took our riffs and lyrics and would practice them with Brian until they were polished into complete arrangements. There were a lot of times in Brian's room at the Music House where we actually sounded like a real band. After the three of us had the tunes down we would try to teach them to Jimmy Shred. It took him about a week to learn just one song. He had no sense of rhythm or melody and his vocal skills were non-existent. But he was good looking, knew how to take control of a stage, and, boy, could he scream. We were playing punk rock, and in the end all that really mattered was that our singer could scream. It took Dave almost as long as Jim to learn the tunes. Even though he wasn't actually playing his bass, he wanted to really practice his moves so people would think he was jamming like a virtuoso. It worked. To the naked eye, Dave was the best musician in the band.

We played a couple of frat parties in the beginning. These were sloppy, loud affairs. We never went on before midnight, and with the exception of Brian, the whole band was usually dead drunk. While not as bad as our first show, these gigs seldom produced a melody, although most of the time we were all at least on the same beat. The frat boys seemed to like us. Granted, they were all too shit-faced to have much of a critical opinion, but sometimes they and their girlfriends even danced. We got more gigs. These were always at parties and we got paid in free beer and a couple of joints. The band usually sounded lousy, but nobody dragged the keg out on us.

Brian's girlfriend, Jenny, began to play keyboards for us. She had never played a musical instrument before, but

Brian wanted to get her involved in his creative project. He began to give Jenny intensive lessons and even worked out a play-by-numbers method for her. He pasted a tiny number onto each of her synthesizer keys and made out a graph chart for every song. Each square on the graph corresponded to a section of the lyrics. While we were on stage Jenny would read along through her charts and press each numbered key when its right time and place came up on the graph. Her synthesizer leads were simple and kind of coldly mathematic. Unfortunately, if she lost her place on the chart, she would play the wrong thing all the way through the rest of the song.

Brian had been in marching band throughout high school so naturally he wanted Third Leg to be a big band. He always wanted more sound, more instruments, more happening on stage. That was the mood of the times: MORE. Me and Pip were really influenced by what the Talking Heads were doing back then. We had been fans since they were a four piece, but now they were completely fleshing out and transforming their sound with ethnic percussion and extra people. They were our heroes and we wanted to be like them. Music was much bigger than just three chords and punk rock. Me and Pip caught a bus up to Manhattan and bought bongos and steel drums from the music stores in midtown. Often, while on stage, Brian would let his drum machine pound away on its own with a pre-programmed beat while he did leads on a tuba or trumpet. We got a second keyboard player. She was an attractive lesbian named Gwen who played fast hip-hopping riffs that laced through the songs and infected them with funk. As time went on, Third Leg developed a sound you could actually dance to. But we never lost our moments of pure nihilistic noise. During our live shows the music began to expand and contract. Sometimes we'd climb complicated scales like stairs that reached florid heavenly highs of complexity. At other shows the tunes never got more intricate than two chords or three loud notes of feedback.

I became a connoisseur of feedback. For a while there I was playing on a gold solid body Fender copy. It had a wah bar that pumped up feedback as easy as water from a well. I would study and chart out where the best areas of distortion were in relation to my amplifier. Often after our soundcheck, I would spend an extra half-hour mapping out the zones of feedback on the stage. Each club sounded different, depending on how high the ceiling was and how far away the walls were. The way their PA interacted with my amp was also a major factor. Even things like carpets and the kind of upholstery on the chairs made a big difference in the brands of distortion I could get. Once I had it all figured out I would plot my coordinates by marking the floor with masking tape and a magic marker. There was such a violent purity to the sound of unadulterated feedback. For some Third Leg tunes I never even touched my strings, just pumped the wah bar and waved my guitar in the air around the amplifier, shaping the lead by chopping through different vectors of noise.

We wrote raw raunchy songs in Third Leg. We were fashionably obsessed with sex, death, excess, and the negative side of the human condition. Like most rock bands, we hated all forms of authority and sang about tearing down the bureaucracies of control. Our tunes had cynical titles like *The Profound Eloquence of Destruction, Media Contamination,* and *Multiple Personality Disorder.* One song called *Why I Need Therapy* consisted of Jimmy Shred complaining about a number of petulant little gripes while behind him played a tape collage made up of clips from TV newscasts. As the tape recorder and Jimmy droned on and on, the rest of the band members would wrestle each other instead of playing. The song *Dance to Armageddon* was about par for the course. It was a three chord rocker with a solid beat that contained lyrics which went:

> *Dance to Armageddon,*
> *Kill every commie red one,*

Gives me traumageddon,
Can't get a hard on,
Party in Saigon.

These were actually pretty sophisticated lyrics for Third Leg. I think Pip wrote that tune. At first, Jimmy Shred wrote all the song words. With few exceptions, his lyrics were completely moronic. Almost every tune he wrote was a love song which proclaimed his strong emotions for one of two things: hot-looking blond babes, or his skateboard. As time went on, the rest of us in the band realized that Jimmy was writing the same song over and over. So bit by bit, me, Brian, and Pip began adding new tunes which had more intelligent lyrics to the set list. The three of us wrote about Nietzsche, nuclear destruction, and the fall of America. By the end, Third Leg's songs were more often about biohazards than blondes. But it's hard to really tack down what exactly we were all about. The band was a living, growing thing. It fluctuated wildly and was impossible to control. Our sound reminded me of an amoeba flowing all over the place and oozing into strange corners. We were musical yet dissonant; complex and at other times simple; sophisticated yet lowbrow. For me, Third Leg was the place where all the many parts of life came together in one roaring whirlwind.

One of my favorite Third Leg songs was *A Morbid Propensity for Explosions*. At some shows we changed the title to *Subtlety*. But anyway, for this tune everyone in the band turned their instruments up all the way until their amplifiers burned into screams of white noise feedback. While the rest of us filed off stage through the shrieking din, Jimmy Shred would stand at the mike, bellowing at the top of his lungs. It was a great song to end shows with.

How did we come up with the name Third Leg? Don't blame me. I didn't pick it. If we'd had it my way the band would have been called something sophisticated, like Immaculate Penetration. But no, we ended up being called

Third Leg. I was always afraid people would confuse us with The Dickies. Picking a name seemed to be harder even than writing all the songs. It was the one thing no one could agree on. As a result, for our first few gigs we performed under a different name each time. Because of this, I suggested we call ourselves The Changelings or The Chameleons but, of course, these titles didn't wash with everyone else in the band. In the beginning, when we were just playing parties it didn't really matter that much. Most of the people at those gigs were too drunk to remember that a band had even played there. But as we approached our first real bar show, me, Pip, Brian, and Jimmy decided enough was enough. It was time to pick a name.

I remember the big trouble-shooting meeting where the whole band decided, come hell or high water, before we left that night our group would have a title.

"How about 'Virgin Potato'?" suggested Pip.

"Dude," said Jimmy Shred. "You all sucked so bad you still live on in infamy. We'll never get a gig if we try to re-use that name."

"How about 'Christian Pornography'?" I said.

"Nah," replied Brian. "My parents are Christians. Some day, when we're playing the Spectrum or something, I might want them to come see us."

"How about 'Cigarette? No. War? Yes.'," suggested Pip.

"Too confusing," I said. "Besides, Pip, you smoke."

"Oh yeah," he said, as if he had just realized it.

"How about 'Skate Or Die'?" put in Jimmy.

"Too cliche," the rest of us said in unison.

"What about 'Catch Them and Kill Them'?" suggested Brian.

"There's already a band called that in Philadelphia," I replied. There really wasn't another band called that, but I just said there was because I thought the name sucked.

"What about 'Pterodactyl Earrings'?" said Jenny. She was wearing plastic pterodactyl earrings at the time.

"No way," shrieked Jimmy Shred. "People will think we're a bunch of posers."

"How about 'That 40-Year-Old Flesh'?" I said.

"Nah," countered Brian. "People will think we're an oldies cover band. How about 'The Adult Cabbage Patch Doll'?"

"What'll we do when cabbage patch dolls go out of fashion?" replied Pip. "We may as well call ourselves 'The Mood Rings'."

"Hey, I came up with a great idea the other day," New Wave Dave burst in. "Look, I found these beside the road." He pulled out a roll of ninety-nine cent stickers. There must have been over a thousand of them.

"What are those?" I asked.

"They're price stickers for bread," answered New Wave Dave. "I was thinking we could call the band 'Ninety-Nine Cents' and now we already have our stickers all made up. We could paste them all over town, on telephone poles, in bathrooms."

"But how will people know that they're advertising a band?" I asked. "Won't people just think they're a bunch of ninety-nine cent bread stickers stuck all over the place?"

Dave thought about this for a second, then smiled and said, "Well, that's extra cool. That way the cops won't know they're advertising a band either."

"Huh?" was the group response.

"How about 'Third Leg'?" interjected Jimmy Shred.

"No way," moaned everyone.

"Aww, come on," he whined. "It's a great name. It sounds macho."

"I don't want us to be a macho band," snapped Brian's girlfriend. "Besides, you guys are big enough dicks as it is."

"Even me?" asked Brian with a hurt expression.

"Everyone except you, honey," she corrected.

"If we wrote that name on a bathroom wall," I said, "nobody would be able to tell it from the rest of the graffiti."

"It's just lame," replied Pip.

"How about 'The Rolling Bones'?" New Wave Dave chimed

in. Brian just made a loud farting noise.

" 'Humiliation Is The Only Pure Emotion'?" suggested Pip.

"Too long," I mumbled. "Wouldn't fit on a marquee."

At one point in the evening we decided to name ourselves after some obscure African tribe. That would make us sound really multi-cultural and world beat. Pip got out his anthropology textbook and we began to go through tribal names, but still nobody could decide on which one to use. So we switched to an English dictionary. We began to randomly open it and point to words. Only this process soon broke down too because nobody wanted to be called something like 'Of', 'Marmalade', 'Dialysis', or 'Floor'.

" 'Follow That Heater'," said Pip.

" 'Twitching Membrane'," I yelped.

" 'The Forjic Turd'," blurted out Brian.

" 'Dime Bags Of Sinse'," squealed Jimmy.

" 'The New Wave Dave Band'," New Wave Dave shouted.

" 'Girls In Charge'," yelled Jenny.

" 'Edible Graffiti'," I suggested.

Pip threw in, " 'Nudes For A Dollar'."

" 'Kid Climax'," cried Dave.

" 'Fart Sandwich'," screamed Jimmy Shred.

Finally, we just wrote all the names out on little pieces of paper, threw them into a hat, and shook it up. We let Jenny reach in and pick the winner. No one was more upset about the winning choice than her. 'Third Leg'.

"When you're born, your parents give you a name, but everyone has a secret name, an inner hidden title which only they know. And my name is The Stranger." The Stranger was a curly headed sophomore who had eaten way too much LSD. It was only three o'clock on a Friday afternoon and he had already consumed two and a half hits.

"Part of a premeditated forty-eight hour binge," he said. "No need to worry, it's a yearly ritual."

I guess the rest of us looked a little squeamish. Me and

Pip had just come over to his dorm with a couple of girls we met at the dining hall to try and score some pot. We picked up the bags from a dealer and were walking out of the all-male dorm when music by The Residents came blasting out of The Stranger's open door. Me and Pip had to go and investigate because we'd never heard anybody play The Residents on campus before. After we said hello to him and talked about Ralph Records for a couple minutes he invited us in to get stoned. That's when The Stranger began to get weird. He showed us thirty hits of acid he had in his refrigerator. Me and Pip tried to buy a hit but he said no way, he planned on eating them all that night and through the course of the next day. It was his 'Annual 48 Hours' as he called it, kind of a rite of passage. He had two bottles of tequila to take the edge off and had already finished a third of the first one. Then The Stranger began to talk about inner names and alternate identities and stuff. The creepiest thing about the whole scene was that he was tripping alone. A few minutes before we left he turned the stereo up so loud we couldn't even hear what he was saying. There was just the booming monster voice of one of The Residents laughing.

Later that night, somewhere around five a.m., he evidently freaked out. He was all alone in his room and took a crowbar to the walls. Managed to pry out about twenty or thirty concrete cinder blocks before turning his attention to the furniture. He smashed all the dressers, chairs, shelves, and bed fixtures into kindling and strew them about the dorm hallways. The next morning the campus police woke him up. The Stranger had taken off all his clothes and was passed out in the middle of the quad, wrapped up in an American flag.

Pip was born and raised in England. He still had a thick accent and obsessively kept track of the London music and fashion scenes in magazines like The Face. His favorite bands were The Jam and The Cure. When he was in ninth grade his parents moved to New Jersey, so he had lived in the US for about four years and his accent was fading. He worked hard at preserving it by watching British movies and TV shows. But still, you could tell the accent was slipping. One night he confided to me, "I hate to say it, but when I get drunk, I talk really American."

Pip's full name was Pippin. His parents called him that because they were big new agers who really got into JRR Tolkien around the time of his birth and decided to name him after one of the dwarves in *The Hobbit*. This, combined with their Catholicism, scarred the boy beyond repair. Is it any wonder people like us turned to punk rock?

One of our first real club gigs was at the Wagon Wheel Tavern. The place was your typical college town bar with nightly drink specials and a good sized dance floor. Its clientele was usually composed of frat boys and rednecks with an occasional influx of suburbanites and old local hippies. This was the Delaware Valley, home of one of the world's stalest music scenes. If you weren't a standard blues band whose set was eighty percent covers and whose originals were so boring and derivative they were indistinguishable from covers, then you had almost no chance of getting a gig anywhere in the area. Except for the alternative station on campus all the other radio stations in the tri-state area of Pennsylvania, Maryland, and Delaware played an endless dirge of classic rock. I had heard the greatest hits of Springsteen, Led Zeppelin, and Aerosmith so many times that I was tempted to go back and burn all the albums of my adolescence into abstract sculpture. The punk rock scene was boiling over on the West Coast and in the major cities around us but in the Delaware Valley uptight club owners kept their doors locked to it. We only got the gig at the Wagon Wheel because Big Bobby Brody sold the owner coke and Bobby convinced him to take a chance on us.

I remember that night well. We got paid a case of beer

(one of our better paychecks) and the soundcheck went smoothly. Before the show me and Pip poured a couple beers into our nervous stomachs. The campus radio station had given us a lot of promo so the club was beginning to fill up to a pretty big crowd. Most of them were just curious, but at least they had come. The dressing room was only a dingy little hole in the wall but it was a room to ourselves. This was a start. About a half-hour before we were supposed to go on Jimmy Shred and Big Bobby Brody came backstage. They had two beautiful blonde girls with them and a large busted brunette. Bobby took the dressing room mirror off the wall and began to lay out fat rails of cocaine. For about ten minutes the room honked and sputtered with a nasal chorus. Then everyone started talking really fast. The blondes, of course, focused their attention on Jimmy Shred, much to the chagrin of his girlfriend, but the brunette complimented me and Pip on how cute we were and how well we played our instruments. Surges of animal energy were ricocheting through my muscles and I thought, yeah, this is alright. This is what being a rock star is all about. Brian Box and his girlfriend sat over in the corner saying nothing. Both of them abstained from drugs and I could tell they were disgusted with our behavior. But what the hell, life's short, and I did another fat line.

All of a sudden, it was time to go on. It still seemed too early, even though we had been sitting in the dressing room for over two hours. As I walked onto the stage with a guitar strapped around my neck my pulse rate was so high my head felt as if it were inflating balloon-like with each throb. For a moment I had a strange fear that my frenzied heart would leap out of my rib cage and bounce off across the stage, forcing everyone to hold up the show while I chased after it. We plugged in, switched on our amplifiers, and turned to face the audience. No stage fright this night. In fact, most of us were so pumped up that if we didn't start right into the jam our bodies probably would have exploded.

We chopped into the first song, *Newark Realty*, at twice its usual pace. Jimmy Shred started snarling out the lyrics,

"I don't wanna drink a Skid Row keg,
I don't wanna pay rent to Scarleg,
I wanna live cross the way,
Wanna hear the knock of Big Bobby Brody."

Out in the audience I saw Big Bobby Brody wince. If there's one thing a coke dealer doesn't want, it's notoriety.

At first the crowd seemed completely baffled. But slowly over the course of the song their strange stares melted into smiles. By the time we hit the psychedelic rave-up after the final chorus we had them. I kept ripping away on a long stream of frenetic notes that laid down a two-dimensional layer of sound like a rhythm track. Then Brian Box put the drum machine on auto-pilot and walked up to the front mike with his French horn. He proceeded to play one of the most beautifully lyrical leads I have ever heard. Here was all this cruel primal grind behind him while he drifted with angels in the clouds. By the time he finished the audience was on its feet cheering.

We leapt from one song to the next and the crowd warmed up with each tune. By the halfway point they were dancing. Towards the end of the set a coke bubble burst in my brain and I took off on a jet engine. As the rest of the band sputtered out on the song *Chas Is Bumming*, my fingers blurred up and down the fret board in an improvisational lead. The thing just leapt through me, as if I was suddenly possessed by the voodoo spirit of Hendrix or something, I couldn't stop it and the sound of my twisting strings went off in a curve over the audience. The rest of Third Leg sank into silence and stared at me. This wasn't on the set list. But Brian thought it was great. He kicked right in with a fast staccato drum solo and the two of us went off like sprinters on the hundred yard dash. With a bit of sardonic glee I realized Brian was trying to catch up with me and I played even faster in an attempt to coax him up to my own drug accelerated speed. The audience and the band watched us go, wondering when it would stop. When the beat got up to the pitch of a whine Brian left the drum machine on automatic and grabbed his French horn. He played a jagged shrieking improv that sounded more like something from Coltrane or Miles than the Ramones. And the whole time I just tried to make the jam go even faster. My consciousness drained out of my body and into my hands, I wanted them to become comets. For about five minutes we kept it up and I put so much into the velocity that at one point I fell onto my back and began to roll around the stage while my hands went on as separate entities. By the time we finally slammed it to a stop the audience was breathless. There was a moment of silence and then the crowd began clapping, they were unsure at first, it sounded like a flock of doves taking off, but the applause gained momentum and then grew to thunder. The band exited through the stage lights, smiling and waving.

Backstage, BBB turned us on to even more coke. We must have gone through two or three grams by this point. "You guys were great," he kept saying. "Just wonderful."

Pip asked if anyone had noticed our set was only twenty minutes long. "Nah," Bobby said in that snow blind voice of his. "They loved you guys."

After an extremely white half-hour the owner knocked on the dressing room door and said it was time for our second set.

We got back on stage and started out with *Newark Realty* again. By the second or third song the audience realized were playing an exact duplicate of our first set and pockets of chuckles and titters erupted here and there throughout the crowd. You see, there was a reason why our set list was so short. Jimmy Shred had a hard time remembering lyrics and he refused to be embarrassed on stage by blacking out in the middle of a tune. Me and Pip had tried coaching him acting-style but his memory was swiss cheese and most of his concentration was directed towards cute blondes anyway.

By the time the Wagon Wheel gig came around we were limited to playing no more than about five songs for the whole show. This meant we really had only one set which we would have to play twice in a row. It was in our contract with the club to have two full sets so we were hoping no one would notice. But, of course, everyone did. By the end of the third song some of the blasts of laughter from certain tables were so loud they momentarily eclipsed the music. Yet after their glee subsided, people seemed to realize that they liked the songs even better the second time around. On top of this, our lyrics were so stupid and simple that the audience had already memorized the words and towards the end of the set they began singing the songs along with us. It's hard to explain the feeling one gets when you're playing on stage and you look out at a crowd that is singing along to your tunes so loudly you can hardly hear the lead singer. This weird occurrence actually turned out for the best because during the last song, when I was supposed to sing along with the chorus, I forgot what the words were and if it weren't for the promptings of the audience I would have been totally lost.

We walked off stage wondering if we should change our name to The Repeats or The Retreads. But once we got into the dressing room the walls began to vibrate as the audience screamed for an encore. Not knowing what else to do, we went out and played *Newark Realty* a third time. The drunken crowd screamed and pounded on the tables, shouting out the lyrics so loudly that our presence on the stage was kind of a moot point.

After the show we went up to the owner of the club and asked if we could get some of the door. Everyone had paid a three dollar cover charge to get in, the place was packed, he'd sold plenty of drinks, and besides, the crowd loved us.

"Sorry, guys," he said. "You only played one set. I don't care if you played it twice. Our contract said two full sets. I don't pay for reruns."

"Yeah, but you pay good money to bands that play nothing but covers," Jimmy Shred interjected. "Our songs are all originals."

"Doesn't matter," the club owner said firmly. "Covers are better than originals. People don't like anything new."

"Says who?" said Pip.

"Says me," replied the club owner. "And it's my joint, so what I says goes. You're not getting paid and that's that."

Jimmy Shred went to take a swing at him but I grabbed his arm and pulled him away. If he hit a club owner we'd never get a gig in this town again. Besides, until we finished paying our dues, the most important thing was just to have places to perform. Even though the club owner was an asshole he was the only person who'd given us a gig so far. We'd probably have to play his lousy joint many more times if we ever wanted to become famous. No use in alienating people from the get go. Sure, he was a royal prick, but we'd probably meet a lot more like him before we ended up on the Billboard charts.

Unfortunately, this turned out to be very true. The road to success is paved with a million assholes and crooks. But we didn't let it bother us that night. On the whole, we thought the gig had been a smashing success. We loaded out our equipment, dropped it off at Brian's place, and me, Jimmy, Pip, and New Wave Dave went back to BBB's apartment and snorted coke until a bright pink sun rose over the happy suburbs of Newark.

It was a Halloween to remember. Chaos went out as Captain Chaos in a superhero costume complete with a tornado sewn onto the chest. Later that night he was so drunk he attacked a dog and beat it half senseless before the animal bit a hole in his arm.

My friend James Shut was smoking a cigarette at a fraternity dance when a girl backed into him and burned a hole in her dress. She and her large football-type boyfriend got extremely pissed and demanded he pay for the dress. Without saying a word James got up and left. The girl and her boyfriend followed him back across campus to his room, insulting him the whole way. James didn't say anything to them. When he got back to his dorm room they followed him in the door. James grabbed a bottle of gin off his dresser.

"You people want a drink?" he said.

"Yes," both of them said snidely. They acted as if it was the least he could do.

James broke the bottle against the wall and shook the jagged end at them.

"Well, I want to drink your motherfucking blood!" he screamed. "I want to drink it and gargle with it!"

They ran. He never saw them again.

That night a girl with long black polished nails scratched me almost every place except for my back. I was getting obnoxious with her at a party so she clawed my arms and chest till the red was spilling. So I backed away and showed her some tongue. In a nanosecond she threw those long fingers into my lips and gouged out the bottom of my mouth. I was spitting blood for fifteen minutes. Later, she was clawing through my shirt so vigorously she broke off the end of a nail. She picked the end up off the floor and said, "I'll kick you in the balls if you don't chew on it." I did. It tasted good.

At another party a construction worker dressed as Ropeman screamed out, "I've been wearing ropes all night and still haven't found someone to tie me up!" In the middle of the drunken crowd, Eve dropped her panties and pissed on a red plastic chair. While trying to pick up a lesbian later that night, I offered to shave off all the hair on my body if I could sleep with her and her bulldyke friend. She was dressed as a wizard and hit me repeatedly with her Freudian wand. Captain Cumulus (Master Of Meteorological Occurrences) threw cottonballs of fog across the room. Chris Catch freaked out and sprayed his face with black spraypaint while screaming, "It's Halloween! It's Halloween!" At night's end, Captain Chaos grabbed a frightened neurotic girl and screamed, "I hate you so much it's love. I want to shave your pubes in the shape of a cross!"

One of Third Leg's first big songs was an anti-sex anthem called *Sex Is Overrated*. We got the song title from a friend of ours who worked as a sperm donor. He hated having sex. He much preferred masturbation, which was good considering the line of work he was in. "The reason I'm doing such a booming business," he said, "is because all those yuppies out there in Suburbia Land are too damn lazy to work on their genetics. Sex is just no fun anymore." The lyrics to the song went like this:

> *Sex is overrated*
> *though no one will state it*
> *Liz Taylor is overweighted*
> *a new man be traded*
> *Reagan's crotch so hated*
> *not even crabs invade it*
> *Kafka masturbated*
> *when he wrote The Trial*

At this point we just had a 'la-la' part and a guitar lead, and then the next verse went:

> *Take your only daughter*
> *to the virgin slaughter*
> *Preachers on the take*
> *rape her on the stake*
> *Blood on her white skin*
> *real world forces in*
> *Torn doll on the floor*
> *Virgin to a whore*
> *Still Daddy's little girl*

Then we just faded out with a chorus of Jimmy Shred singing "Sex is overrated," over and over. You have to remember that this was like 1980-something. Nobody in Delaware had even heard of AIDS yet. Nobody thought sex was overrated.

Except the sperm donor.

Inevitably in every jam session, despite the booze, endless tuning up, bong breaks and other mind clouding diversions, there came that moment everyone had been waiting for. Pip called it the point where you "let the coolness get down to your vertebrae." That time when all the random chords, notes, and feedback would smooth out into a distinguishable throbbing riff, a killer hook that everyone playing recognized and understood, and they surrendered all their individuality and the ego of their leads to the contours of the sound. The guitars and keyboards hooked onto it like surfboards and as a band we rode the wave. The groove became so complete that we let our eyes roll up into our heads and our bodies shake with it. Suddenly everyone in the jam session played as one note, one sound. You couldn't even tell what part your instrument was playing in it all until you stopped and could hear where your emptiness diminished the whole. Jenny said when we were totally caught in a groove like that it sounded as if someone was singing even though there was no one at the microphone. Those were the moments that made us gather together every week to sing our songs. Not the beer and bong hits, they were the mere residues of a search for spirituality. But the true zen came when we all hit that sync, when five people and their instruments in a smelly basement suddenly became one and our minds went blank and were taken over by some higher force. In those days of disbelief it was the closest you could get to religion, and there was a kind of angel in the ringing of our ears.

In high school I stretched the tether of my parents' rules, but did not break it. At college things accelerated. I felt like an acrobat climbing precipitous nets of stimulants, socializing, studies, LSD dawns spent screaming at empty cars, mohawks and leather, vague war clouds and Nicaraguan mines, slam dancing, a shadow of nuclear missiles, Picasso, Seurat, and comic books, women's faces over plastic glasses of beer, rising with their warm bodies on rainy mornings, all nighters, pressures, satoris screamed into sunsets, and a creeping sense that the murky strands of things would knot into one big rush, but what would happen and who would I become?

We had already been to three parties, drinking at least our two beer minimum at each one. If it doesn't get good after two beers, it's not going to. This party seemed middle of the road. Frat boys, preppies, and denizens of mall culture. At least they still had a heavy keg.

"Can you imagine if laughter was spontaneously regenerating?" I asked. "One giggle would keep growing till you suffocated to death."

"Comedians would be executioners," said Jimmy Shred.

"You'd have to make the world so bleak," added Pip. "People would walk around whipping themselves whenever they accidentally heard a joke. Or if someone started to laugh everyone around him would have to beat the shit out of him to save his life."

"Can you imagine a primitive tribe in the jungle where some god walked out of the trees and laid down the prophecy that laughter was taboo and deadly?" I said. "Man, the first anthropologists to find them would flip."

"They wouldn't flip," said Pip. "They'd probably start laughing at them."

A few feet from us some already drunk frat boy drank a half gallon of Budweiser from a beer bong.

"Man, that reminds me of some guy I knew in junior high school," said Jimmy Shred. "His name was Dave Gene. Both his parents were major alkies. But anyway, we had this big party for him at his house on his seventeenth birthday. We fed him twenty-nine straight shots of Wild Turkey till he was sittin' all alone on the couch in his basement, vomiting down his shirt into a beach pail on his lap. Then, just when he was reaching maximum hurl, everyone at the party lined up across from him in this sadistic choir and began singing a twisted version of *Happy Birthday To You*. Dave was so fucked up he couldn't even kick us out, just sat there puking on himself and giving us the finger."

We all drank to that story. "Have you all seen Chaos's new girlfriend?" Pip asked.

"That woman is a skeleton," I said. "She can't weigh more than ninety-five pounds."

"Chaos likes 'em anorexic." commented Pip. "He told me once that he loves it when their knees touch before the thighs."

"But she's such an airhead," Jimmy Shred complained.

"Eve calls her 'Fluff'," I said.

"I don't think there's even that between her ears," replied Jimmy.

"She hates my guts," said Pip.

"How come?" I asked.

"I'd had a couple too many at Brian's party last week," said Pip. "And I told Stacy Glanmug that Fluff was so offensively preppie and ignorant I honestly felt she was the only girl on campus I wouldn't fuck. I said that the carnal energies which went into the production and sustainment of her metabolic functions could have been much better spent in another fashion. I didn't realize it, but her and Chaos were standing right behind me. He laughed; she went red and started screaming, 'Dance for us Pip! Dance for us!' "

"Why'd she say that?" I asked.

"Oh, Eve says that for someone who loves music so much, I have no sense of rhythm and dance like a one-legged centipede."

"You foreign freak," Jimmy Shred said with a smile.

"Hey, but we Englishmen have cute accents," he replied.

"I think a Bronx cheer sounds better," Jimmy Shred laughed while lighting a fart with his butane lighter. The flame shot out from his butt like an orange chainsaw.

"Man, I saw the weirdest thing on the way back from the beach this weekend," said Pip. "We stopped at some choke-

and-puke diner for a snack. It was a sleazy place. Greasy truckers, dime store whores, and hard scrambled eggs. But anyway, we're waiting for our food and there are these two tables of gay deaf mutes trying to pick each other up. There were about ten of them. All of 'em making obscene pantomimes like jerking off empty air and pretending to stick invisible dicks in their mouths. They were going on and on in the crudest fashion but they were hardly making any sound at all. It really freaked me out. And then when I got up to leave, out in the parking lot, there's this van painted all dark purple, and on the side it says 'Varicose Van' in red letters shaped like veins."

"Well," I said. "Even gay deaf mutes need love. And you know what they say, 'Sex is just a physical outgrowth of love.' "

"Nah," Jimmy Shred replied. "Crabs are a physical outgrowth of love."

Suddenly, who should walk into the party, but Chaos. By the time he had grabbed a beer and pushed his way through the crowd to us, me and Pip were debating philosophy. We were discussing how emotions shape our overall perception of reality. I was illustrating one of my points by describing an old girlfriend of mine.

"The first time I ever slept with Jill I thought of her as just another lay. She didn't turn me on that much at first. I thought a lot of her weight fell out of the wrong places and her face seemed like a banner of ignorance. My first impression was that she was an incurable airhead. But then our friendship grew and soon matured into something bigger. I found out I had been completely wrong. She was extremely intelligent, maybe even more so than me, and on top of that she was hilariously funny. Then one morning I was watching her get dressed. Her movements were so graceful and when she looked at me and the light hit around those gentle shadows on her face making them all velvety and I thought she was the most beautiful woman I'd ever seen. Around that time, whenever we went anywhere, I picked roads that had a lot of people milling about. I wanted to show her off. But after our arguments I couldn't look at her. Her face would go rigid and all the warmth in it would run away and these little wrinkles would huddle between her eyebrows. She seemed clumsy and I thought, 'Damn, I'm going out with this dog?' Physical attractiveness is a purely emotional perception."

"Bullshit," said Chaos. "What about Miss December? I think she's beautiful and I don't even know her."

"You think she's beautiful because a multi-million dollar industry has developed prefabricated standards to warp your view of natural attraction. You think she's beautiful because Hugh Hefner tells you so. That's the way corporations work, isolate you from your real feelings and then make you pay for their aesthetics."

"I don't care if she's only three dollars worth of paper. I'll still whack off to her, I love her," replied Chaos.

"There's more to life than whacking off," Pip commented.

"Yeah," said Chaos. "There's money, too."

"You're incorrigible," I muttered.

"Yes, and rich some day as well," he quipped.

"Chaos, it's people like you who are making us into another lost generation," I said. "Gimme my paycheck before they drop the bombs. Everybody just wants to fuck and do coke while the babies by the waste dumps grow extra legs. Slam dance to Armageddon!"

"You make it sound so complex," Chaos said sheepishly. "I'm just greedy and raised on dreams of middle class mediocrity."

"If you fell in love you might mutate into a human being," Pip said to Chaos. "I mean, you change your fucking personality monthly. This fall you were a punk rocker, last year you were a frat boy, then you thought you were gay, then you went straight again, now you're a preppie. What next?"

"A neo-Nazi botanist," he replied. "I want to send minorities off to concentration camps and force them to grow marijuana."

"Hey Chaos," I said. "Where's Fluff?"

"She kind of drifted off," he mumbled.

"There was some dude in my hometown who fucked a '57 Chevy," Jimmy Shred said, changing the subject.

"Bullshit," whined Pip.

"No shit," insisted Jimmy. "It was at a big bonfire party. There must have been about a hundred people there and then he pulls off the cap and starts fuckin' the gas tank. And we yell, 'Joey! What the fuck are you doing?' An' you know what he yells? He yells, 'I've fucked everything else here, I may as well fuck this, too.' "

"What a freak!" yelled Pip.

"I may have met my match," said Chaos triumphantly.

"Whatever happened to him?" I asked Jimmy.

"About two months ago he stole a taxi. They caught him over in Maryland. He was on his way to shoot the president. Yeah, Joey was a real psycho. I remember this one time a couple of years ago where he was running around the local bike shop screaming, 'I'm the Antichrist! I'm the Antichrist!'. And some customer in the shop yells, 'Prove it!' so Joey starts screaming, 'Cause I got 666 carved on the end of my dick!' "

On that note we all headed back to the keg and filled up another round. As we were walking back through the living room there was a knock on the front door. Chaos went to answer it. He pulled open the door and asked the people standing there, "Is Chaos home?" After a couple seconds of confusion they just walked past him into the party. That was the way Chaos used to answer his phone back then, too. Whenever it rang he would pick up the receiver and ask "Is Chaos there?" instead of saying "Hello." He said he tried to time it so that he was asking "Is Chaos there?" at exactly the same time as the other person was saying it. "It's just like stereo," he said. "Sometimes it freaks people out so much they get scared and hang up the phone."

I noticed Chaos was looking a little down so I pulled him

aside and asked him what was going on.

"I don't know," he said. "Tonight it was dark and windy. Should have rained but all the clouds kept getting blown to pieces. I was sitting on this bench and all these people were walkin' by. You know, the kind you used to talk to at parties and in bars a few years ago but now the social drift has blown you so distant that you just nod and smile at each other in public and go 'Hi so-and-so' and keep walkin' in your own direction. And all these people kept walkin' by, all my failures, and I was nodding like a goony bird. I'd negated them, and myself along with them. I began to get sad. Haunted by a memory I couldn't remember. Something far out in the night, touchless, out of reach.

"It's like, when I was a kid I got lost one night in the woods by our house. Usually, I could find my way home by the light on the back porch. But there was this black mist all through the trees; must have been from the coal factory. Who knows? Maybe the porch light was just burned out. But in any case, I was lost for hours, and ran and clawed my way through the underbrush, submerged in my fear, covered by it like weeds till the terror took me over and became me. I was screaming and crying but it was late and no one was awake to hear me. I didn't know if I'd ever see that beautiful sixty watt lightbulb again."

"So what happened?" I asked.

"Finally I fell asleep on some moss and woke up in the pink light of dawn. But now I feel like I'm in those woods again. I lost something. I don't know where. Maybe it was in all the girlfriends I've gone through, maybe it was in the chemistry all of us used to have. The old conversations. But it's gone. And now I feel like I'm living with one leg instead of two. Things aren't bad enough to be worth killing yourself, but you don't run anymore. It's not just that I don't know what I want, I don't even know what I want next, or if what satisfied me all along was really what I desired or just an illusion. Something I thought I wanted but it was only a mirage over something hiding, sliding away whenever I reach out to touch it."

"You want to get stoned?" I asked.

"Got any cyanide?" was his reply.

"Just cigarettes," I answered. "Want one?"

"Yeah, I'll take some of that weed too. What kind is it?"

"Primo sinse," I said.

"Solid."

I lit up the joint and we puffed on it for a couple of minutes. The lazy blue smoke drifted around our heads as the languid atmosphere settled into our gray matter.

"So Fluff's history?" I asked.

"Pretty much," said Chaos.

"Man, you go manic depressive every six months and it only lasts till you get fucked again."

"That's a bunch of shit," Chaos snarled adamantly.

"How long's it been?" I asked.

"Three weeks."

"See, two weeks past when you get DTs and uncontrollable erections."

"Man, that's not it," Chaos protested. "I'm not interested in fucking. Well, I'm interested in it but I don't need it. I've had enough that it's not what I really want anymore."

"What you want is Fluff or a facsimile that looks just like her."

"Man, that's all over and I can deal."

"Yeah, you can deal, but you don't want to. You want something that strong and you want it now cause you need it like a junkie fix. What? You think perfect relationships grow on trees? You think the world's your own private suck machine?"

"Lay off," Chaos threatened.

"No, I won't lay off," I said. "You and Fluff had a good thing. It was a relationship with real tenderness. Both of you were fuckin' joined at the waist, if you two were any softer you would have been a lump. Lots of people never have that. So you two had a good thing and now it's over. So you move on. That's life; moving on till you can't move no more. Nothing lasts forever. But at least you two got to rest for a little while. You got to stop and see the world frozen in its spastic dance. And you weren't alone. For a while you weren't alone."

"I know," Chaos said dejectedly. "But why did it have to end?"

"Fuck why," I said. "Only neurotic closet masturbators like Nietzsche worry about that. Everybody else is to busy learning dirty jokes so they can get picked up in bars. You ought to live up to your lip service and concentrate on getting to someplace in life where you don't ask a lot of stupid questions."

"But where am I now?" Chaos whined.

"Who cares?" I said. "Where are you going?"

"I don't know," Chaos said. "I definitely feel like I'm drifting. It's like some huge mysterious wave is carrying me far away from everyone to a strange wanderspace."

"Shut up and smoke the rest of this joint," I said, bringing the conversation back to the safe realm of the superficial. "You've seen too many Bergman movies."

"I know, but histrionics are good for picking up chicks," Chaos said smiling.

"Fuck chicks," I said. "I think I'll just buy a cat. The only shit they give you is in a litter box and they meow real loud when you hump 'em."

God, I thought to myself, I can't believe I just spent five minutes convincing Chaos that he needs to be more superficial.

I remember our first big radio interview. It was on Jess the Jam's show on WDOA. Jess worked at a local record store and had once slept with our extra keyboard player, Gwen, before she figured out she was a lesbian. Somehow they had managed to remain friends and he always gave her great discounts when she bought records at his store. Third

Leg had already begun its meteoric rise through infamy by the time Jess asked Gwen if the band could come into the station for an interview and do a live, on-the-air performance. Of course, we were all ecstatic about having our noise drift out through those invisible radio waves.

WDOA was the college radio station. It was one of the few stations in the country that had developed a strong alternative rock program. They were the first people in Delaware to air the Maximum Rock'n'Roll show which was taped in Berkeley. In the mornings the programs were jazz, folk, and classically oriented, but from three in the afternoon until late in the evening the DJs spun the new sound. The first time I ever heard industrial music was on DOA. The same with gothic rock, ska, and death metal. That station really broke a lot of new ground. Each of the alternative rock DJs had their own unique style and tastes in music and all of them were good in their own way. For example, there was Chip, the industrial DJ. Chip loved noise, the uglier the better. His favorite bands were Throbbing Gristle and Einsturzende Neubauten. One time he devoted an hour of his show to a tape recording of a chain saw trying to cut through an iron girder. Another time, while doing his show under the influence of LSD, he played an entire side of a Renaldo And The Loaf album backwards at 78 rpm. Chip was constantly getting kicked off the air for playing albums that contained profanity and explicit descriptions of sex.

Jess the Jam, on the other hand, was much more sedate. He liked music that actually had form and structure. His favorite bands were X and The Gun Club. Why he liked us I'll never know. We were one of the noisiest, worst, most unstructured bands around. But Jess liked everything. His album collection had jazz, classical, even country and western records in it. He gave everybody equal time and never turned down a request.

Because the studio was too small to accommodate all our instruments, we decided to play an acoustic set. This would also cut down on the problem of generating too much feedback in an enclosed space. I, of course, stated that too much feedback was never a problem but this was one time when I was voted down. Back then I was a strict theorist. I didn't even own an acoustic guitar. "If it can't be distorted then it has no relevance to the future of music," I said during our discussion of what we should play on the air.

We all gathered in front of the station at four in the afternoon, and Jess let us in. He showed us how to use the mikes and we set up our limited equipment and did a soundcheck. Then after fading out a Ramones tune, Jess spoke into the mike with those mellifluous tones of his. "Well, everybody," he said. "I've got a special treat for you all today. Yes, it's none other than those notorious outlaws of rock and roll, Third Leg, here in the studio today with yours truly, Jess the Jam. Why don't you all say hello to everyone out there in TV land?"

"But if they're watching TV how will they know we're on the radio?" New Wave Dave said with a confused look on his face.

"Hi everybody in Radioland!" the rest of us screamed.

"And I think you all are going to do a song today for us, aren't you?" said Jess.

"Yeah," said Jimmy Shred. "This is an easy listening version of our big punk rock hit, *Fudgepacker*."

Me and Brian started strumming a couple of acoustic guitars and the rest of the band joined in on a choir-style version of the tune. It actually sounded pretty good, a little too mellow for me, but the chords were so absolutely solid and catchy you just had to sing along. After we were done Jess began the interview.

"What are some of your major musical influences?" he asked.

"The Bee Gees," said Brian.

"Bands that lip sync," said New Wave Dave.

"The noise of big factory machines, or maybe the sound

of crickets at night," said Pip in his most fashionably cool British accent.

"I always liked Fleetwood Mac," said Jenny.

"The Dickies," said Jimmy Shred.

"Is that what made you all chose the name Third Leg?" asked Jess.

"No!" everyone but Jimmy shouted in unison.

"Well, how about the rest of you?" asked Jess. "What were your influences?"

"Patti Smith," said Gwen.

"My affinity for electric guitar," I said, "began at an early age when I licked a wall socket and nearly electrocuted myself to death."

"Well," said Jess. "That's interesting. What about drugs? Do they play a big role when you all are composing your music?" The thought of calling what we did 'composing' made half of the band burst out laughing. "No, I'm serious," insisted Jess. "Do you all use drugs?"

"Got any good drugs?" asked me, Pip, Dave, and Jimmy simultaneously.

"Uh, no, not really," said Jess, not really knowing how to respond.

"We were going to smoke a joint on the air today," said Jimmy Shred. "But then we realized it wouldn't make enough noise, and since nobody could see it they wouldn't believe we were actually doing it."

"Thank you for not smoking," said Jess. "I have horrible allergies. I'm allergic to the FCC."

"What about you, Jess?" said Gwen. "People say you're addicted to different scenes. They say you walk around town with a bottle of hair styling gel in your pocket so you can change your look to fit into a blues, preppie, punk rock, or redneck party. Rumor has it you're such a social chameleon that by the end of the day you have a grease buildup in your hair that's so big it takes half a bottle of Janitor In A Drum to shampoo it all out."

"Gwen, if I didn't love you so much I'd smack you on the air right now," said Jess. He reached over and pressed a button on the sound effects board. There was the sound of someone getting their face smacked followed by a tape of Moe of the Three Stooges muttering, "So you think you're a wise guy, do you?"

"But seriously folks," said Jess. "What is it that Third Leg hopes to achieve? Fame? Stardom?"

"We wouldn't mind quitting our day jobs," said Brian.

"Yeah, I'd love it if some big record company would just send me fat checks in exchange for living in a recording studio for the rest of my life making funny noises," I said.

"But you all must have something you're trying to prove," insisted Jess. "Some kind of political statement the band is trying to make. I mean, I've been to a couple of your shows and you're completely different from everything else that's out there. I don't know whether you're better or worse than the competition but you're certainly unique. What is it you're getting at? Are you trying to carve out a whole new sound?"

"We're going for the sound of giant praying mantises eating school buses on the New Jersey Turnpike," I said to the DJ. Everybody stopped and looked at me for a second. Then the interview went surging on.

"No, we sound like the Incredible Hulk doing a rail slide on a rad ass skateboard," yelled Jimmy Shred.

"We sound like good coke," New Wave Dave exclaimed.

"Like dead babies," hissed Pip in a gothic rock sneer.

"But if we sounded like dead babies," said Jenny, "we wouldn't make any sound at all." Everybody stopped and thought about this for a moment. New Wave Dave seemed to be pondering it especially deeply.

"I guess you're right," Pip said kind of quietly.

And then Jimmy Shred pulled the ultimate radio faux pas. "Hey Jess," he asked the DJ. "Isn't it true that you dye your hair? And not only that, but it looks like you've dyed it so much it's beginning to fall out. Are you going bald,

Jess?"

The DJ was stunned. There was an awkward silence. A long dead space in the radio waves. And then the DJ started making these spitting sounds. Saliva was spraying all over the microphone. If he kept it up we were sure to get electrocuted. Luckily, Gwen instantly saw how to smooth it over with her feminine cool.

"Who cares?" she said. "He's still the cutest."

Jess the Jam instantly began to calm down, and a few seconds later even let a smile spread across his face. "I will say this for you guys," the DJ sighed. "You're definitely the most assaultive rock band I've ever interviewed."

"We take that as a compliment," replied Pip.

"How's about another song?" suggested Jess.

We launched into an acoustic version of *Blonde Gash*, one of Jimmy Shred's I-want-to-fuck-this-blonde-haired -girl-so-bad-my-dick's-about-to-leap-off-my-body-like-a-model-rocket tunes. It was one of our catchiest riffs at the time and may even have had pop hit potential. Unfortunately, every other word in the lyrics was 'fuck', 'pussy', or 'cock'. Jimmy was hardly ready for writing Hallmark cards. So in order to keep Jess the Jam from getting kicked off the air we did the tune as an instrumental. No only that, we did it as a kazoo instrumental. For the next five minutes WDOA sounded like a nature show studying strange birds. All of us were out of time with each other. Personally, I've always thought kazoos create one of the most annoying sounds that exists in the natural universe. Evidently, lots of people agreed with me. Listeners were calling up to complain before we had even finished the song.

"You know," Brian said to Jess as the DJ slipped in a Cramps tape to quiet the masses. "We've done a lot of shows and people always hate us. Even when we're good and play in tune, there's still a certain percentage of the audience who can't stand us. It's kind of weird, trying to make art which you find a certain beauty in, but which everyone else always misunderstands and finds ugly."

"Ah, don't sweat it," said Jess. "It always takes people a long time but eventually they'll catch on to what you're doing. Hell, in a few decades, even pure dissonant noise like feedback or drills grinding into metal will become so accepted people will be playing tapes of that kind of stuff as elevator music. Besides, every band needs a gimmick. With the way punk rock is turning everything on its ear these days, you all's greatest claim to fame may be the fact that you can make people hate you."

It happened after slamming with the skinheads at the Stiletto Sex punk show where the lead singer was wearing an extension cord for a belt and plugged it into the wall as a joke and electrocuted himself. Afterwards we went to Troy's Diner. This real twinkie of a girl was talking to a guy on the phone when her boyfriend walked in and heard her whisper into the receiver that she loved him. Her boyfriend's face kind of fell in and he turned and punched his hand through the quarter-inch glass of Troy's front window, then took off running out the door and down the street. The two bruisers that made subs grabbed a baseball bat and a two-by-four, and ran after him screaming, "Let's Party!" Me and Jimmy Shred ran after them to watch the blood fly. The dude ran down the street a block and into Doc's Pub where he tried to hide in the bathroom. When me and Jimmy ran in, the bouncer asked for a two dollar cover charge. "We're just here to see them beat the shit out of the guy that broke the window two doors down," we said. The bruisers from Troy's dragged the boyfriend through the crowd, had his head in a full nelson and were trying to break his neck. There was blood all over the boyfriend and he smeared everyone he brushed against. Once outside, the bruisers threw him on the sidewalk and started kicking him till the bouncers broke it up. The end of the boyfriend's thumb was hanging by a little piece of flesh and his forearm was wound in wide gashes of spongy red with veins poking out of 'em. There was blood everywhere. He was laying on his back begging, "Just don't call an ambulance! Just don't call an ambulance!" When the dudes from Troy's went to call the pigs he began walking down the street going, "Leave me the fuck alone!" and would have disappeared into an obscure night world of street lights, but the guys from Troy's caught him again and brought him into the back room of the diner where they began to pulp him because he couldn't afford to pay for the window. We could hear him groan every now and then as we sat out front and finished eating our meatball sandwiches.

Another one of Third Leg's best gigs was the Student Center Show. It was a night of alternative music sponsored and heavily promoted by the campus radio station, WDOA. Four bands were on the program and through some act of God (and blatant brown-nosing of one of the DJs by Pip), Third Leg landed the opening spot of the night. With each show Third Leg got bigger. By this time we had Pip on bass, Jimmy Shred on vocals, New Wave Dave on backup vocals and bass, me on guitar, Brian on drums, French horn, guitar, and just about anything you could pick up that made sound, Jenny on keyboards, Gwen on extra keyboards, and for this show we added a new guitar player named Sparky Bruno. Sparky was a solid, musically trained guitarist who Brian hoped would help anchor down a sound that all too often had drifted into the eye of a hurricane. As the band progressed my guitar work got increasingly bizarre. I couldn't seem to get over my deconstructionist leanings. Sometimes I played nothing but feedback through an entire show. I loved to play leads using a vibrator as a slide, it shook the strings with such an eerie sound. Other times I just helped Brian with the rhythm by laying my guitar on the stage and pounding the strings with steel wrenches. I think I already sensed that the band's days were numbered and there was a subconscious drive on my part to take things as far out there as they could go. This made for great stage antics, but it left things lacking in the sound department. So we drafted Sparky into the band to hold down a steady rhythm guitar. He also played great psychedelic surf leads and sang backup vocals. This left me free to do what I had always wanted to do - sit on the edge of a stage and make funny noises.

Me and Pip hung out by the back door of the Student Center, shared a joint of good green bud, and a few minutes later we were on stage. We went straight into a maximum rocker called *Slug Daddy* that was dissonant, fast, and atonal. By the end of it people were already heckling.

"You suck!" some high school kid screamed.

"Just let the French horn guy play," yelled someone else.

"Get off the stage!"

Jimmy Shred turned around. He looked scared. "Look, we're going straight into *No Cops*, okay? One, Two, Three!"

No Cops was one of our best and tightest songs. It snatched us away from the jaws of doom. The chords were fast and furious and they yanked people out of their chairs. Within the span of a minute the floor in front of the stage occluded into a churning slam pit. People jumped in the air and flew over each other's shoulders. By the time the last chord slapped shut we had recaptured them. Unfortunately, by that time I had also broken all but two of my strings. There were only two spares in my guitar case and one of them was a duplicate of a string that hadn't broken. But I put both of them on anyway. Jimmy Shred didn't know what was happening and went straight into the next song. Only half the band followed him, but when he refused to stop the rest of the musicians joined in. Dave was the one person considerate enough to wait for me. In the middle of the song Brian put the drum machine on automatic and came over and helped me restring and tune my guitar. There were only four strings on the axe but they would have to do. It sounded twangy and strange, took a little getting used to, but by the next song I was up and running. We charged through the rest of the set, the audience was splashing waves against the stage, echoing moans of feedback filling up that concrete room, notes scrambling beneath my fingers like squashed ants. When Sparky played his surf leads the little girls squealed and cooed, keyboard riffs flew past quicker than laser beams, and the whole time the slam pit arched and rolled, grinding muscles slapping against muscles, people rising into the air as if the electricity in our amplifiers were disintegrating gravity itself. I remember during the last song the hardcore riffs took everything over, our arms and mouths exploding in sonic blasts, people diving and jumping as if their flesh had become chaos, and the music demon possessed Pip so totally he threw down his bass, strapped on a crash helmet, and jumped headfirst into the crowd.

Third Leg had a lot of fans but one fan I could have done without was Sara the Vegetable. We also called her The Thing. Sara had the lumpy playdough body of an adolescent and big round glasses that were as thick as ashtrays. She was a clinical schizophrenic and she followed me everywhere like a revolting shadow I couldn't seem to shake. Her schizophrenia made her mind a jumbled opaque soup where understandable sentences only occasionally rose to the surface. These statements were often ludicrous to the point of hilarity but they were few and far between. Most of the time she would just sit there watching with an unnerving crab-like stare. The Vegetable's stare had an unending fascination that let you know there was no conscious thought behind it. When Sara sat down at people's tables in the dining halls she would silently ogle them until they were so nervous and upset that they got up and left. She tried to cling to social groups and cliques like a crab lice. Every day Sara would sit down with them in the dining halls even though she was uninvited. Most people would politely ignore her but after awhile Sara was so omnipresent you had to recognize her existence. Usually when this happened the clique would start to gibe and tease the Vegetable, taunting Sara for her strangeness and social ineptitude. Eventually their constant insults would sink into the girl's dim brain and she would move on to another group. Members of groups who had already been plagued by Sara described her as a kind of social disease.

Third Leg and their entourage used to hang out at a long table in the Student Center dining hall. One day Sara simply sat down and joined us. After she had been with us a few minutes, Jimmy Shred nudged me and whispered, "Hey, who's that weird-looking girl sitting at the end of the table?"

"I don't know," I said. "I've never seen her before. Who does she know?" When we asked people about her after the meal it turned out she didn't know anyone.

But the next day she was there again. And the day after. And the day after that. Nobody said a word to her, everyone completely ignored her, but she kept showing up. When she showed up for lunch on Friday all she had on her tray was two bowls of strawberry and lemon jello. "Hey," said Jimmy Shred to her. "How come that's all you're having for lunch?"

"I only eat primary colors," Sara replied.

This was only the first of a long list of famous Sara the Vegetable quotations. One night at a party she told me that during one of her more severe schizophrenic bouts, "Everything became solid. My whole world turned to concrete." Another doozy was, "Light bulbs are really deformed fireflies." And, "Oxygen is really blue, it's just that people's eyes can't see it."

Since she was an art major most of her bizarre statements referred to color. Such was the case with everyone's favorite Sara quote, "Time is orange." Third Leg and our circle of friends liked this statement so much that one year we all went to a Halloween party dressed as Sara the Vegetable. We wore glasses made from the bottoms of Coke bottles, dumpy clothes, and our watches were nothing but round pieces of orange construction paper tied to our wrists. Sara was at the party too and didn't know what to make of us. Whenever she asked us what we were dressed as we would reply, "We're you, Sara. That's what Halloween means. As soon as you put on a costume the rest of the world turns into you." My friend Keith Bethany liked Sara's weird quotations so much that he eventually typed them all up and published them as a chapbook.

Nobody really liked Sara. She was a constant annoyance. We tried to expel her from our group with constant taunts and teasings but for some reason she clung to us more tenaciously than she had other cliques. I guess she sensed that we were one of the few crews on campus strange enough for her to ever gain acceptance in. But Sara was too weird even for us. Only we couldn't get rid of her. Verbal abuse went right through her without even registering. All of us were pacifists and never would have considered physical violence so after a while we just learned to tolerate her constant hovering presence. This awkward situation was further exacerbated by the fact that she always showed up at the parties we went to. Nobody ever invited her or told her where the festivities were occurring but she always seemed to figure out their location through some kind of subliminal osmosis. Even when we tried to deliberately keep a party from her knowledge she would still show up, nice and early, knocking at the front door. Usually we were too polite to send her away.

All this caused real problems for me because Sara had a tremendous crush on me. I never encouraged her in the slightest and at times was downright obnoxious to her in unsuccessful attempts to repulse her attractions. But nothing seemed to work. She followed me around constantly like an embarrassing buoy stuck in my magnetic wake. Even when she had me cornered at a party she couldn't verbalize anything, just stood there and stared at me with those arthropod eyes. After a while I began to wonder if Sara was a manifestation of my bad conscience. She would follow me to and from classes. Unless I was careful to surround myself with people, she always tried to sit next to me at the dining hall. No matter where she ended up taking a seat, she would stare at me throughout the whole meal. God, it made me sick to my stomach. What made matters worse was that this was one of the most sexually active years of my life. I had girlfriend after girlfriend, dozens of one night stands, I was in a rock band, fairly good looking, and getting laid just seemed so easy. After awhile I couldn't even remember all the faces and names of the girls I had slept with. You have to remember that this was before AIDS, herpes hadn't hit the mass media yet, and most girls at U of D were on the pill. People partied a lot more back then. It was before twelve-step programs. Most of these girls I picked up in the drunken kitchens of Skid Row parties, and almost always Sara the Vegetable was there, standing about ten feet away, watching me like a TV camera. Sometimes she would follow me around the party, short-circuiting my pick-up attempts until I just turned around and screamed at her to leave me alone. Her response was always the same: silence and uninterrupted staring.

I remember one night I got picked up at Skid Row. Sara left the party at the same time and followed us all the way back to my dorm. She kept an even pace about twenty feet behind us. When the girl I was with asked who she was and what was her trip, I said, "Look, she's some psycho who's obsessed with me. But I have a plan..." I told her my room number and the combination to the front door of the dorm. When we got to the library we split up and sprinted around opposite sides of the building. Sara was left there not knowing which direction to go in. She eventually decided to follow me, but she wasn't very fast and I easily outdistanced her. Me and my date sprinted across campus and met up at my dorm room. About twenty minutes later, while we were in the middle of having sex we heard a light tapping on the locked front door of my room. We immediately stopped and got dead quiet. The tapping continued. For the next half-hour the tapping continued at intervals of ten to fifteen seconds while me and my date sat there in horror. I felt like a character in an Edgar Allan Poe story. Finally, the Thing stopped tapping and I could hear her walk off down the hallway. I peeped through my curtains and watched Sara exit the front of the dorm and fade off into the early morning darkness. By this time my date was a complete nervous wreck and we never did end up making love. I had had enough.

When I saw Sara the Vegetable the next day I told her if she ever followed me around like that again I would beat the living shit out of her. "You're a psycho," I said. "And I hate your fucking guts. I'll never feel anything but disgust for you, so stop following me around. If you keep it up I'll mess you up. I mean it." For the first time, I think Sara actually heard me. I didn't see her for two days. Those were two of the happiest days of that year. On the third day she showed up again but she kept her distance. Over the course of the next few weeks she gradually drifted off to the periphery of my life like a disturbing dream or memory.

Eventually Sara the Thing slept with Keith Bethany. He picked her up one night when he was dead drunk. "She just followed me home," he said. "So when we got back to my place I fucked her. And it was so weird. She didn't say a word the whole time, but when she came she pissed all over my dick." Keith hasn't been able to get rid of her since then.

Not only was Brian Box all the real musical talent in Third Leg, he also owned most of the equipment. The mikes were his. So was the PA. About halfway through our career Brian went out and bought a full drum set that served us till the end. His girlfriend played his keyboards and synthesizer. I managed to break my guitar and burn out my amplifier from excess volume early on. For a lot of gigs and practices I borrowed the guitars of friends in the music scene. But after awhile I developed a reputation for being hard on equipment. So what if I set borrowed guitars on fire on stage a couple of times? It hardly melted their enamel. I always polished them up real good before I returned them. After awhile no one would loan me their stuff except Brian.

When we played this gig at a fraternity party and Pip had so many glasses of beer poured on him that his bass shorted out and nearly electrocuted him - well, you guessed it, from there on in he played Brian's old Washburn hollow body. And if we needed to hire a sound man, more often than not, Brian paid for it. He wanted it that bad. He thought Third Leg had the spark that could propel us to the big time. He didn't want to end up just being a band teacher at some high school. Like the rest of us, like everyone who's ever picked up an air guitar, he wanted to be a rock god.

One of the things that caused tension in Third Leg was the fact that both me and the bass player, Pip, had a crush on Gwen. This situation was further exacerbated by the fact that Gwen was a lesbian. Only she didn't look like a stereotypical lesbian. Except for her short hair, she was utterly feminine and very desirable. I think in our heart of hearts, me and Pip thought she must really be straight. But in reality she had been living with her present girlfriend for over a year. I used to always flirt with her but she politely brushed me off. Pip would give her little gifts like flowers and candy. Gwen thought these were sweet but she wouldn't give him the time of day. Some of our practices were filled with quiet aching for her. But even our most well orchestrated protestations of love prompted nothing more than a mood of complete disinterest on Gwen's part.

That winter me and Pip went to a party at Gwen's house. This was when Third Leg was at its zenith and we were riding high on a tide of local popularity. Gwen and her lover lived with a bunch of other crazy new wavers in a house on Skid Row. When we got there the place was decorated with black lights and blown-up condoms that had been spraypainted with fluorescent paint. In honor of a Third Leg tune, the affair was dubbed the Sex Is Overrated Party. Since it was a Friday night, me and Pip had dropped acid. We dropped acid every Friday night. It was cheaper than drinking beer or smoking pot. We only drank beer if it was free. A huge blizzard had hit the area and had effectively shut the town down. As me and Pip walked through the drifted snow, soft cars skidded past us like ghosts of metal. We were already tripping so hard the snowflakes looked more like fireflies than ice.

When we got to Gwen's, the house was big, warm, and throbbing. Everyone looked so silly. The beer was free so me and Pip drank lots of it. For awhile I talked to some new wave viper girl in the kitchen. She was almost six feet tall with a tight sinewy body. I don't remember exactly what I said to her, but at some point she hauled off and began kicking me in the balls. I curled up in pain and started to roll away, but she still managed to gouge my neck to bleeding with her long red nails before I scampered out of the room. I figured that my problem was that I hadn't drunk enough to find my manners and went back to the keg for a refill.

After tapping my cup I ran into Pip. He was so sauced he was talking like he had been born and raised in New Jersey. Me and him began to flirt with Gwen right in front of her girlfriend. We were so drunkenly honest that we often made direct statements about how much we wanted to sleep with her. Gwen's girlfriend stood there trying to look like she wasn't paying attention to us. I think she didn't know whether to be flattered or disgusted. As I continued to vocalize dreams of amorous interludes with Gwen, I noticed how attractive her girlfriend was. In my addled mind I began to think that if I struck out with Gwen I could always try and score with her girlfriend. After a clumsy and claustrophobic half-hour the two girls managed to ditch us, and me and Pip bounced around the party like a couple of entropic pinballs. 'What do I care if I'm an asshole?' I thought. 'I'm a rock star.

Rock Stars are supposed to be assholes. I can't wait until Third Leg goes on tour and I can start destroying hotel rooms.'

By the time me and Pip finally came to rest, we were in the attic bedroom. It was here that we found a full bottle of tequila. The seal hadn't even been cracked. We, of course, did the honors. Only we didn't have any mixers or chaser. No problem. We'd just chase straight shots with beer. When the keg went dry and our glasses were empty we drank the liquor straight. Ordinarily, this much alcohol would have put us out of commission, but the LSD we had eaten kept charging us like an electric generator. Pip found some old lime slices in a dusty corner of the room. Someone had already used them for shots earlier in the evening. All the juice was sucked out of them but there was still some meat left on the rinds. Fuck it. Me and Pip started sucking on the limes after doing our shots. At one point a couple of girls wandered into the room and saw what we were doing.

"Eeewwh," said the blonde one. "That's sooo gross. Who knows whose mouth has been sucking on those? You could get some horrible disease."

"Well, at least they won't get scurvy," her friend said.

When me and Pip were done with the bottle of tequila we realized the party was over. There was only silence and a smell of stale beer all though the house. "Hey, let's go downstairs and try and pick up Gwen and her girlfriend again," said Pip. We clomped down the stairs and tiptoed up the hallway to their room. Figuring surprise would be the best method, I pushed against the door. It was locked. I put my ear up to the keyhole. Inside, I heard quiet, gentle, sounds. Someone made a soft moan.

"They're fooling around," I yelled to Pip. "Right on the other side of this door. Two beautiful girls entwined in sexual passion." Instantly, me and Pip began pounding on the door.

"Let us in," we cried. "We want to watch! We mean that in the most respectful way. We're straight guys but we don't mind if you're gay. We won't ask to join in. We just want to watch!"

Suddenly the lock came undone and the door flew open with a gesture of chilling anger. Gwen stood there in her nightgown, her face focused sharp as an ice pick. I walked towards her with open arms. She lifted up a can of spraypaint and graffitied a squiggly black line all over the front of me. I fell backwards, just on the stench of the fumes. The door slammed shut and the lock rattled back into place. The black paint snaked diagonally across my face and I lay there on the floor looking like a renegade from a minstrel show. Pip helped me to my feet and we quietly left the house. Time to call it a night.

The blizzard had raged throughout the course of the party and now the whole world was white, soft and muffled. The town was completely deserted as we walked through it in the three a.m. chill. We talked of philosophy and the snow glowed down. I had decided to crash on Pip's couch that night. It was a two mile walk to his apartment and toward the end we couldn't feel our feet. The wind was howling like all the LSD demons from a bad trip. As we passed the electric sign on the bank it claimed the temperature was minus four degrees. Near the entrance to Pip's apartment complex a blast of polar wind kicked up a sandstorm of snow. It rolled over us in granular waves. For the last couple of blocks we couldn't see more than five feet in front of us.

I woke up on Pip's couch the next afternoon with the worst hangover I have ever had. The slightest movement sent slivers of glass through my brain. I moaned for help but no one was there, all the roommates, including Pip, must have gotten up and gone out while I was passed out on the couch. So I crawled into the bathroom for some aspirin. Unfortunately, the medicine cabinet was empty except for a dusty toothbrush that looked like it had been there for two decades. So I crawled into the kitchen to get some food. When I opened the refrigerator all that was in it was one forty ounce bottle of Colt 45. I screamed in pain and slammed the door shut. The mere sight of alcohol was enough to make me vomit. For almost five minutes I fought back the gag reflex. Even once I left the apartment I had to stop every hundred feet or so and sit in the snow for a couple minutes until I had the strength to continue walking.

That night, Gwen called Jimmy Shred and told him she was quitting the band and I realized I was already a bigger asshole than most rock stars will ever be.

The moment came later in the jam session. Every couple of songs the three guitarists would stop and tune up with their electric tuners, and the keyboardist, the drummer and the vocalist would sit around twiddling their thumbs, looking very bored. Finally Jimmy Shred looked up and said, "You guys, always playing with your tools."

To which I replied, "What is civilization but the use of tools?"

Much of that time period seems like a blur now but one party in particular stands out in my brain. Often, when Third Leg had written a few new tunes, we would throw a party just so we could try the new material out in front of an audience of guinea pigs. Our parties were notorious. Chemicals abounded, alcohol lubricated everything, and even if your genitals didn't get a workout at least your mind would get fucked. All the local punks, skinheads, and new wave girls showed up at our parties. This soon created a social inertia that dragged in the rest of the social outcasts. We did everything we could to make the atmosphere free and open. It worked. Soon we were the favorite band of the local gays, hippies, blacks, scattered ethnic types, and all the other groups that didn't quite fit in to the oppressive monochromatic social scene hanging over Newark like a layer of LA smog. Our parties were the mixing zones where people woke up the next morning having slept with someone they thought they would never even speak to. This one party was the zenith of that whole melting pot time.

It was a Saturday night and Third Leg was jamming in the corner of Helen's living room. Because it was the first weekend in April we had decided to throw a Halloween party to confuse people. But the word didn't get out properly so only about a third of the people there had actually dressed up in costumes. One gay couple came as Siamese Twins. They both had pierced tongues that were attached to each other by a long gold chain. Unfortunately, as the evening went on and their inebriation increased, they developed a tendency to walk away from each other to chat with someone on the other side of the room. This brought many conversations to a rude ending. I stood up in front of everyone with my eyes closed, feeling the LSD in my arteries bleed out into the guitar strings. All I could hear was voices and distortion. When I opened my eyes I saw a dwarf from India dancing with a black man over six feet tall. Against the far wall I saw a bulldyke making out with a drag queen. So I just closed my eyes again and kept that music flowing out into all their moving bodies. Our tunes whipped them back and forth, the new material went over great. It was warm and humid as a kiss in that room, the party seemed so safe and friendly, a secure haven from the ugly prejudices drifting through the town around us.

We ended the set and walked into the crowd covered with that good sweat, the kind you only get from creating things. Someone handed me a beer, I gave my girlfriend of the moment a kiss. This was youth and life. I couldn't stop smiling as I talked to my friends. Over on the couch Chaos was sniffing glue with Ted the Skinhead. They went through at least a half-dozen paper bags before they switched to paint thinner. Chaos would pour about two teaspoon's full into the bottom of the bag, close the opening around his nose and mouth like an oxygen mask, and suck in and out until all the fumes were gone. A little later our friend Keith walked into the party and it was obvious from his syrupy speech that he was very drunk.

"What are you all doing?" bubbled Keith.

"Paint thinner," Chaos replied with just the right touch of cold eloquent decadence.

"Can I try some?" Keith asked in a brainless voice.

"Sure," Chaos replied and handed him the bottle of thinner.

Before anyone could do anything, Keith had unscrewed the top of the bottle and was guzzling down the thinner like it was water. He managed to swallow almost a third of the contents before I grabbed the bottle out of his hand.

"Jesus, you idiot!" I yelled. "If you want to take the enamel off your throat why don't you try sandblasting?"

A cloud of paranoia drifted across Keith's face as he realized what he had done. Chaos, who had been in these situations before, merely hustled him into the backyard so he could throw up.

"That's what you get for drinking too much," commented Pip, who had watched the whole thing transpire.

I grabbed another beer and wandered through the party. By this time the crowd appeared to be mostly gay. Effeminate boys squealed at each other. One guy was wearing a leather cowboy suit that had the ass of the pants cut out. Over by the coffee table was a man dressed as a giant cucumber. It was such a wild scene that I was just grooving on it. But it was too good to last.

A couple moments later our friend Maria ran in the front door crying. "This group of five guys from the football team followed me all the way here," she sobbed. "They were making horrible comments the whole time, but I ignored them completely and just kept walking. Then when we got to the front of the apartments, they grabbed me and tried to hustle me into the bushes. I think they wanted to rape me! I just started screaming and punching at them. One guy had me around the waist and was trying to pull my pants down, so I scratched at his eyes with my fingernails. I must have got him pretty good because he groaned and let go of me. Then I ran in here. But they're still right out there!"

I pulled open the front curtains just in time to see a barbaric display of macho assholism. The electric company had been working on the power lines that week and had left a few spools of wire lying around. These spools were as big as a coffee table and weighed over two hundred pounds. Outside the window I saw one of the football players with a spool of wire lifted over his head like King Kong holding a boulder. With a pea-brained roar he threw the spool at the front door of Helen's apartment. When it connected, the flat plane of the door instantly became a concave wreckage of splinters. The reaction was instantaneous. All the men in the room stopped their sweet conversations, flexed their muscles, and moved as one towards the front door.

As Chaos pulled at the handle, the whole thing fell to pieces and he leapt out into the darkness. All the other men in the room filed out after him. By the time we caught up to the football players they were in the parking lot. Chaos sprinted in the lead. He didn't wait for any prompting, just jumped like a crazed hyena onto the jock who had thrown the spool, and began punching at his face and biting his shoulders. Chaos was a blur of snarling vicious force. The football player screamed out in real terror and by the time he managed to throw his attacker off of him Chaos's mouth was full of flesh and blood. Chaos had never turned around to see if anyone was backing him up - he just went into action. But when the football players turned around to face Chaos, they saw the biggest wall of angry pansies they had ever seen in their life. Fear leapt from one football player to another as they realized how outnumbered they were. There was even a giant cucumber out there flexing its fists. One effeminate queen screamed, "We're gonna do us some ass kicking," in a lisping high-pitched voice. The football players looked like they wanted to melt into the ground. I could almost hear their assholes tightening. Chaos stood in front of them panting, just waiting for the carnage to begin. "We're going to bust some heads!" screamed the guy standing next to me. I looked over at him. He was wearing a white t-shirt that had a huge bar code on it with the words 'Generic Faggot' written underneath.

But the showdown never came down. Because as we stood there two police cars drove up and four armed officers jumped out. "There they are! Get 'em! They were gonna kill us!" yelled one of the football players. A cop just walked up to him and slapped on the cuffs. Then they handcuffed the other football players and pushed them into the back of the squad cars. One of the cops asked if anyone wanted to be a witness. Chaos and the Generic Faggot volunteered. It turned out that Helen had called the police as soon as Maria walked into the apartment. Leave it to the women to deal with things in a civilized fashion. People began to mill back towards the party. Some of the gay men cast off their gruff stances and voices and resumed their light effeminate gestures. Almost everyone was talking about how we would have "really kicked their asses." At times they sounded just like a bunch of redneck yahoos. The squad cars drove off. In the backs of them the football players almost looked relieved at getting arrested.

Third Leg's greatest hit was a punk rock anthem called *Fudgepacker*. This tune spawned the band's best and worst moments. It had a killer four chord riff that cut right through the bullshit to your spine and made you dance. It started out heavy and slow with lyrics that snarled over the top like broken glass icing. Measure by measure it built in speed and complexity. Each verse was faster than the one before it and the whole thing just kept going up up up until it all broke out in the fastest psychedelic rave-up the East Coast had ever heard. At most of our shows it was either the last tune or the encore.

Me and Pip had written the music but Jimmy Shred

penned the lyrics. Although he was kind of a dick, Jimmy wasn't prejudiced. A number of people in his inner circle were gay. There had been some gay bashings on campus. Even though he was straight, Jimmy Shred had often been taunted and called faggot just because of the company he kept and because he had a funny haircut. So he wrote the lyrics to *Fudgepacker* as a way of speaking out against the violence and prejudice. The words went something like this:

> *Fudgepacker, stay away,*
> *Fudgepacker, you're gay.*
> *Fudgepacker, chased away,*
> *rednecks beat you up today.*
> *Get out of here you fucking queer,*
> *scream the assholes drunk on beer.*
> *Words of hate make the whole world stink.*
> *Words of hate from people who never think.*
> *It's gonna end the world sometime,*
> *names that split instead of combine.*
>
> *The words we use when we abuse*
> *are the ones that make us fools.*
> *They're a person like you or me,*
> *looking for love and company.*
> *Love don't have a specific shape,*
> *and when it comes your way*
> *you'd better take it.*
> *Come on fudgepacker, don't go away.*
> *Come on fudgepacker, stay, stay, stay.*

The tune was just so catchy you couldn't keep it down. It spread faster than a cold. I used to walk around campus and hear people humming it to themselves and singing, "Fudgepacker, stay away..." Which was part of the problem. Like most big songs, people only remembered the first couple of lines of the lyrics. With just those two sentences taken out of context it sounded more like an anti-gay song than an anti-discrimination anthem. This problem was further complicated by the fact that Jimmy Shred screamed out his lyrics when he sang so it was hard to make out what he was saying. I told him to be more clear when he sang but it's hard to change someone's style. Other times the soundboard mix at our shows was so muddy it was hard to understand the lyrics. To a certain degree, I also believe that many people, when they go to a show, don't listen to the words anyway. They may listen to the sound of the singer's voice, but they don't really tune in to what he's saying. The painful truth of all this was driven home for us one night when me, Pip, and Jimmy Shred went to a drunken townie keg party. Most of the night the three of us just stood around whispering to each other about what a bunch of prejudiced, lowbrow bastards this crew was, but we stayed there because the beer was free. Then later in the evening a bunch of rednecks began loudly putting down homosexuals. It became sort of a game with them, to see who could degrade gays lower into the ground. Me, Pip, and Jimmy couldn't believe the ignorance and hatefulness we were witnessing. Suddenly all the rednecks broke out singing the chorus to *Fudgepacker*. They proceeded to sing the entire song, only they had a completely twisted and wrong version of the lyrics. It came off as a grotesque hate anthem. I don't know if they had honestly misunderstood the words or were deliberately warping the lyrics to fit their own hatred. It didn't really matter. It was our song that was causing the damage. The three of us looked at each other and a profound spiritual nausea flowed through us.

"What have we done?" said Jimmy Shred. "What have we created?"

But probably the most interesting *Fudgepacker* event happened a couple weeks later. It was a Saturday night and the whole band was practicing. Besides the jam, we had no other plans. During a break Brian got a call from one of his music friends. The friend had gotten us a gig at a party. The catch was that it was the party he was calling from right then and if we wanted to play we had to load up our stuff immediately and drive straight over. Brian said sure, no problem. A gig's a gig. We piled all the equipment into my stationwagon and headed out.

The party was in an apartment complex outside the city limits. We walked in, not knowing what to expect. Well, we got more than we bargained for. It was the gayest party I have ever been to. I didn't experience a scene like this again until years later when I moved to San Francisco. The place was packed and it was one hundred percent men. And flaming they were, too. At odd intervals the room would literally erupt with squeals and shrieks. Many men were walking around in nothing but their underwear. In one corner I saw seven men engaged in a group kiss. Guys were making out all over the place. It was totally Boy's Town.

We carried our equipment in and began to set up in the living room. Every time one of the guys in the band bent over to plug something in they got pinched on the butt. We'd swat them away, but it was useless. The pinches returned quicker than horseflies.

"Oh, a band of cute young punk boys, here to entertain us," squealed some queen lounging on the couch. "How scrumptious. Are you going to play cover songs from *The Boys In The Band*? Or how 'bout some show tunes? Maybe you want to back me up while I do my impersonation of Barbara Streisand?"

"Sorry," Pip said. "We don't do covers. We're an original rock and roll band. We're hardcore."

"Well, honey!" shrieked the queen. "At least something around here's hard."

The living room was pretty small, only ten by ten feet or so, and most of that was filled up with furniture. We tried to spread out the equipment as best we could, stacking it on easy chairs and along the couch, but most of our amplifiers ended up facing each other and being only a few feet apart.

We had no mixing board. It was a soundman's disaster.

While I was out at the car hefting another amp, Jimmy Shred ran up to me. "Man, everybody at that party's gay," he whispered.

"So?" I said.

"So how are we going to play *Fudgepacker?*" he asked in a panic.

"It's a pro-tolerance song," I stated.

"Yeah, but what if they misunderstand the lyrics, like all those rednecks at that townie party a couple weeks ago?"

"Just make sure you sing clearly," I replied soothingly.

"Yeah, right," he said. "Man, even when we have a soundman at a state-of-the-art board people can't make out exactly what I'm saying. In a place like this, with no mixer or PA, hell, they'll hardly understand a word I'm singing."

"So what are you worried about then?" I asked.

"Well, they'll probably be able to at least understand the chorus. 'Fudgepacker, stay away, Fudgepacker, you're gay.' I mean, what if they think we're trying to put them down? They might..."

"Might what?" I asked.

"I don't know. Try to gang buttfuck us or something."

"You're paranoid," I said. "If it bothers you that much, we can just skip that tune tonight."

"But it's our best song!" exclaimed Jimmy Shred.

"So why don't you change the lyrics around a little," I suggested. "To something that will suit the crowd."

"No way," Jimmy said firmly. "Nobody messes with my lyrics. My words are my art. I don't let anyone censor them. Those are the words I wrote, those are the words I'm gonna sing."

"Have it your way," I said.

That living room was a hot claustrophobic space packed to capacity with men. It smelled like a locker room, breezes of BO wafting over us as Third Leg stared them down. We were sweating profusely before we even began playing. Then came the moment of truth. We switched on the power and went into the first song. Our amps were so close together that all of them instantly began to feedback with this eardrum-piercing hellspawn scream. Only Dave's amp didn't feedback, and that was because it wasn't even plugged in. To keep up appearances though, Dave bent down, turned his volume knob up all the way, and kept shaking his bass in front of the speaker to make it look like he was helping create the noise. About all we were making was noise. But the band played on anyway. Jammed our hearts out while our eardrums melted. A monotone cry of feedback was constant through every song, a sound so loud it eventually brought the cops down on us. There were many times during the show that the distortion blowing out of Pip's amp beside me was so loud I couldn't even hear what I was playing on my own instrument. Much to his chagrin, Jimmy Shred's vocals were one of the few things you could hear clearly. But I gotta give him credit. The boy had balls. He sang all his tunes straight through without changing a word. When we got to *Fudgepacker* he sang it just as it had been written; he didn't even hold back when he belted out the chorus.

And the crowd? Well - they loved us. In fact, they went ape shit. They acted like we were the hottest thing since toast. Granted, we were mostly a bunch of good-looking young boys and they might have just wanted to jump us, but who cares? Fans are fans. Don't question their loyalty or adoration. All across the room in front of us they were jumping and cheering like a bunch of hormonally-crazed teenage girls. Whenever Jimmy Shred turned away from them for the slightest moment, someone would reach out of the crowd and goose him on the ass. I remember at the end of *Fudgepacker*, as Jimmy was singing, "Fudgepacker, fudgepacker, fudgepacker," over and over again, one of the gay men right in front of him turned around, pulled down his pants, and stuck his butt out at Jimmy while squealing,

"Ohh, pack me, honey! Pack me!"

Third Leg's most memorable performance was probably the State Theater gig. We were the opening act before the fifth anniversary showing of The Rocky Horror Picture Show. For those of you who don't know, The Rocky Horror Picture Show is a cult movie classic that encourages audience participation. People throw food, spray water, scream obscenities, and dress in weird spaceman drag while acting out their own psychodrama versions of what is happening on screen. It was a good gig because we knew Third Leg would be playing to a packed house, but there was a catch. "The Rocky audiences are out of control every week," the manager of the State Theater told us. "Because it's the fifth anniversary they're going to be particularly rowdy. I wouldn't wear my best clothes up there."

"What are you getting at?" asked Jimmy Shred.

"I'm saying there's a good chance you might get things thrown at you," the manager replied.

We assumed the worst, of course. So when the band got ready for the gig we set aside a stock of water balloons, paper towels, and squirt guns. Pip ended up performing that show in a rain poncho. But I took the whole thing a little bit further. I was working part-time at a dining hall on campus and had a dinner shift the night of the show. One of my duties was to throw out the uneaten food. The main course that night had been Salisbury steak in gravy. It wasn't a very popular entree so I had ten trays of it to pitch into the dumpster. Only none of the food went into the trash. Instead, I filled up a green plastic garbage bag with the steaks and gravy, and took it to the show. By the time we went on they would be ice cold. It's a brutal world, I reasoned, so it's important to have a strong weapon of defense.

We were rather nervous backstage at the State Theater. The natives were ugly. A couple of eggs had been thrown at the stage before everyone had even gotten in the front door.

It was a sellout crowd and all of them were drunk. We could smell the fumes on their breath all the way backstage. Like most of our gigs, this show paid us in beer and we were busily sloshing it down in an attempt to drown the butterflies in our stomachs. But it wasn't working. The audience sounded more like a lynch mob than people who wanted to be entertained. We had our weapons hidden behind our amplifiers. The green plastic garbage bag next to my guitar was already leaking a little brown fluid. The band drank in silence. New Wave Dave was happy and upbeat though. After weeks of pestering her, his Mom had finally come to see one of our shows. She was out in the audience right then. Among those animals. Eleven-thirty rolled around. The theater manager came back. "Okay, you guys are on," he said.

"Ladies and gentlemen: Third Leg!"

It was like a strange dream when we hit the stage, all that noise, all those people. Popcorn had begun to fly though the air before we even plugged in. The band surged into *Newark Realty*. The tune went tight and smooth with just the right amount of feedback. By the end the popcorn flying through the air at us was a steady drizzle. The audience seemed poised on the edge of an explosion. "It's time for *No Cops*," Jimmy Shred said. *No Cops* was a crowd pleaser, and always got people up off their asses. I flew into the chords with my distortion totally cranked, a blistering metal sound that melted like butter on a frying brain. Instantly, the audience erupted into pandemonium. People jumped over chairs and rushed to the front of the stage. Each bang of the drum was a whiplash into the slam pit that spiraled up before us. People were leaping through the air, diving off the PA, twisting and bouncing around on the jostling heads. As the song got faster the pit grew more violent. Fist fights broke out. It looked more like a brawl than a dance. There was blood. I saw some skinhead stumbling off with a huge gash in his forehead. For a couple minutes the rain of food slowed down.

It was during the third song that the trouble began. Halfway through my big feedback lead at the end of the first chorus my amplifier made a horrifying sizzling sound and then went completely dead. I tried fiddling with it but soon realized I had blown the speaker. In the meantime, I noticed the drums had disappeared. I looked over at Brian who was tinkering with the drum machine with a nervous look on his face. Because he was afraid his full set might get damaged, Brian had decided to play this show using just his electronic drum machine and a single stand-up snare. Only now the drum machine had gone out. I ran over to him.

"What's wrong?" I asked. "Where'd the beat go?"

"I don't know," he said. "I think the batteries might be dead."

"Don't you have any spares?" I implored.

"No. I forgot to bring some. I was too busy buying squirt guns."

In the meantime, the lack of rhythm and guitar had caused the tune to degenerate into a thundering cacophony. By the time it sputtered to a halt everyone still playing was following a different beat. Brian half-heartedly banged into the fourth song using just the snare but there was only so much he could do with one drum. Besides, the snare was undermiked, so as soon as the other instruments kicked in the beat was lost in the tidal wave of amplified sound. This meant the band had to keep time by intuition. As one might expect, every tune from there on in was all over the place. To add insult to injury, during the fourth song there was a power surge at the sound board which blew out half the channels and the stage monitors. The end result was that out of seven people on stage only three were coming through the mix. The rest of the band emerged mercilessly from the sound board as erratic blasts of dissonance. Nobody on stage could hear what anyone else was playing. Everyone was playing in a different beat. Big chunks of food began to fly through the air. Slices of pizza, half-eaten submarine sandwiches, paper cups full of Pepsi. My guitar didn't work at all. For a while I pretended I was still playing even though I wasn't making any sound. Me and New Wave Dave did a duet. His bass didn't even have a cord attaching it to his amplifier. But his Mom didn't know that. She must be proud, I thought.

The crowd got more violent. Fist fights were everywhere. People began to clamber onto the stage and tear apart our equipment. Pip had stopped playing and was shooting at them with a squirt gun full of colored water. I got tired of pretending to play and ran along the edge of the stage hitting people with my guitar. When the band lurched into a deformed skeletal version of *Fudgepacker* I jumped down into the audience, and using my guitar like a huge phallus, began to bone people in the ass with it.

Food was coming down on us in thick hailing sheets. Rotten fruit and vegetables, toast, beer cans, and a steady mist of popcorn and Milk Duds. The stage was already covered. Our clothes were soaked with ooze and sticky sugar-based drinks. It seemed as if everyone in the audience was throwing edibles at us all at once, like a spray of machine gun fire, a comestible barrage. I ran back up onto stage and grabbed my Doomsday device -the garbage bag full of Salisbury steaks. I dragged it over to Jimmy Shred's mike which I noticed was one of the few things still coming through the mix. In mid-verse I snatched the mike away from Jimmy and screamed, "Eat shit you bastards, and it's real!" I began to lob handfuls of Salisbury steak into the audience. They were dark brown and slimy - they certainly looked like poop. The panic was immediate. People began squealing in disgust. Wherever one of my steaks landed an empty circle was immediately formed. People dived over chairs to dodge them. Unfortunately, one of them hit Dave's Mom square in the face. And not only that, but they brought out the real anger in the crowd. Bottles began to fly with the food. I didn't think it was possible, but the amount of garbage they threw at us actually doubled in volume. At times, the downpour was so heavy I could hardly see the audience through it. By this point the music had completely disintegrated into a confused wave of feedback and distortion. Occasionally, you could hear a guitar riff or one of Jimmy Shred's hoarse and screaming vocals, but these were few and far between. It was pretty much just a solid wall of noise. Half the band had already jumped off stage to wrestle with people in the audience.

One image I will always remember from that show was Brian Box standing on stage in the rain of food at the end, next to his broken drum machine. In an attempt to have his drum be heard Brian had pounded on the snare so hard he had finally broken the skin. Even then he had persisted by banging away on the rim until his drumsticks broke. To be completely silenced is a difficult thing for a real musician. You have to understand that Third Leg was Brian's vehicle, it was his dream. Third Leg was the band that was going to take him to the top, that would get him a major record label deal. The band that would allow him to make his living doing what he loved - playing music. And now he stood there silent, with the dream coming apart before him, with the public's derision, expressed in food, falling all over him, soaking him to the skin. He looked so forlorn and dejected standing there with one broken drumstick in his hand. And as I was watching him a huge jumbo-sized tub of popcorn came spinning through the air and landed directly on his head. The snowy white kernels spilled down the front of him as the cardboard tub came to a rest over Brian's wretched countenance, completely covering it like a helmet. He merely reached his hands up, touched the cardboard tub, and without taking it off, shook his head back and forth in a gesture of infinite sadness.

When I talked to Brian about it a couple years later he told me the State Theater gig was his favorite rock show of all the ones he'd ever played. "Are you kidding, man?" he said. "I loved it! That night was total bedlam! Most rock bands work for years to create a scandal like that. We did it without even trying. It was total anarchy. That show was so crazy I don't know if you'd even call it a rock concert. Maybe performance art is more accurate. I felt like I was one of those Dadaists back in the twenties. Just a full frontal assault on the audience. Most bands are so bland they can't get any kind of a reaction out of a crowd, not even dancing. My god, by the end of that show we were actually wrestling with our fans. I don't know if it was music, but it certainly was rock and roll."

Third Leg abruptly came to an end later that spring. By then Brian owned all the instruments in the band. He got a good job offer to be a high school band teacher in southern Maryland and decided to take it and move there. So one day he was gone and we had no instruments left. We still had some enthusiasm but there was just nothing to play on. The only person with any equipment was New Wave Dave who had a bass but no amplifier so that wasn't much good. We had a couple of meetings to try and brainstorm a solution to the dilemma but it seemed to be a pretty intractable situation. Finally we came to accept our silence and Third Leg was dissolved.

It wasn't that bad. Summer was coming and we all had new places to move to and new lives to drift off into. Our old songs went with us, haunting murmurs in the backs of our heads, tiny cries deep down in the marrow of our bones.

Word is a word so similar to world.

manic d press
publications

Specimen Tank. *Buzz Callaway.* $9.95

The Verdict Is In. *edited by Kathi Georges & Jennifer Joseph.* $9.95

Elegy for the Old Stud. *David West.* $6.00

The Back of a Spoon. *Jack Hirschman.* $6.00

Mobius Stripper. *Bana Witt.* $8.00

Baroque Outhouse / The Decapitated Head of a Dog. *Randolph Nae.* $6.00

Graveyard Golf and other stories. *Vampyre Mike Kassel.* $7.00

Bricks and Anchors. *Jon Longhi.* $8.00

The Devil Won't Let Me In. *Alice Olds-Ellingson.* $6.95

Greatest Hits. *edited by Jennifer Joseph.* $6.00

Lizards Again. *David Jewell.* $6.00

The Future Isn't What It Used To Be. *Jennifer Joseph.* $6.00

Acts of Submission. *Joie Cook.* $3.50

12 Bowls of Glass. *Bucky Sinister.* $3.00

Zucchini and other stories. *Jon Longhi.* $3.00

Standing In Line. *Jerry D. Miley.* $3.00

Drugs. *Jennifer Joseph.* $3.00

Bums Eat Shit and other poems. *Sparrow 13.* $3.00

So Much for Passion. *Wendy-o Matik.* $3.00

Asphalt Rivers. *Bucky Sinister.* $3.00

Solitary Traveler. *Michele C.* $3.00

Into The Outer World. *David Jewell.* $3.00

Night Is Colder Than Autumn. *Jerry D. Miley.* $3.00

Seven Dollar Shoes. *Sparrow 13 Laughing Wand.* $3.00

Intertwine. *Jennifer Joseph.* $3.00

Feminine Resistance. *Carol Cavileer.* $3.00

She Knew Better. *Wendy-o Matik.* $3.00

Now Hear This. *Lisa Radon.* $3.00

Bodies of Work. *Nancy Depper.* $3.00

manic d press
box 410804
san francisco ca 94141 usa